NORTHFIELD BRANCH
847-446-5990

D0571484

KATE ALICE MARSHALL

VIKING

VIKING
An imprint of Penguin Random House LLC, New York

First published in the United States of America by Viking,
an imprint of Penguin Random House LLC, 2023

Copyright © 2023 by Kathleen Marshall
Interior art © 2023 by Matt Rockefeller

Visit us online at PenguinRandomHouse.com.

Library of Congress Cataloging-in-Publication Data is available.

ISBN 9780593526453

Printed in the United States of America

1st Printing

LSCH

Design by Anabeth Bostrup

Text set in Georgia

For my family: I love you dearly.

You bunch of weirdos.

CHAPTER 1

Charlie Greer was nothing special.

Charlie had known from the time she could talk that the world was full of things wilder and stranger than most people could ever imagine. Her parents worked for the Division of Extranormal Research and Investigation, after all, dealing with all the strange and inexplicable things—extranormal things— in the world. That meant everything from ghosts and lake monsters to witches and weird science to mysterious disappearances.

Then there was Charlie's mother. She could see what was hidden, know what was secret, even catch glimpses of things that hadn't happened yet. You couldn't have a mom like Leigh Greer without knowing there was more to the world than met the eye.

For a while when she was very young, Charlie had been convinced that she had inherited her mother's gifts. She had run her fingers over the treasures in the local antique store, certain that she *felt* something, a whisper of memory clinging to wood and tin. She had picked her dreams apart for meaning and tried to match them to the things that happened when she was awake. She was sure, oh so sure, that she was special, too.

"We'll see when Grandpa Rupert visits," her mother had told her, snuggled up in bed at night. "He can always tell." And she tapped Charlie on the nose and smiled.

Then Grandpa Rupert arrived, tall and white-haired, smelling of licorice and wool. He'd looked down at her, suitcase in hand, and said, "So this is the girl. Entirely ordinary, then."

And Charlie crumbled.

Mom never let on that she was disappointed, but Charlie saw her behind Grandpa and saw the way her smile faltered, just for a moment.

A few months later, Mom and Dad brought Matty home. Matty was special. So was Opal, who drifted in the door the next year, the light shining right through her. And Gideon, who arrived the year after, four years old and already making books fly off the shelves when he threw a tantrum.

"You and me, we don't have any special powers," her dad told her, sitting under the shade of the old oak tree in the backyard. "Heck, when I got assigned to the Division, I didn't even believe in all this stuff. But in all the cases your mom and I have worked, we did it together. As partners. Not having powers doesn't mean you can't do amazing things."

"I guess," she'd said, digging a toe into the dirt. He put a hand on her knee.

"Listen. People like your mom and your brothers and your sister, they can do amazing things, but the world is a very dangerous place for them. It's the job of people like you and me to look after them. And that's pretty special, too."

So Charlie worked hard to keep her family safe. She checked the fire extinguishers to make sure they were always full, in case Opal had a panic attack. She sat outside the basement door and read stories to Matty during the full moon while he barked and scratched at the walls. When all the spoons in the drawer were bent into pretzels, she sighed and got the plastic ones from the cupboard and didn't give Gideon a hard time. And she told herself over and over again that she didn't mind being normal.

Sometimes she almost believed it.

Something smashed against the wall outside Charlie's bedroom as she pulled on her socks. The smack was followed by the distinctive sound of shattering glass, and then an angry growl. Charlie sighed as she pulled her red hair up into a sloppy ponytail. Hopping over her abandoned lacrosse stick and backpack, she hurried out into the hall. Her brother Gideon stood outside, hands balled into fists, glaring at her other brother, Mateo. A picture frame, glass broken, lay against the wall, answering the unspoken question of what had made the sound. Charlie glanced at the nail where it had been hung on the opposite wall.

"What now?" she asked, signing to Matty, who was Deaf, as she spoke.

Gideon did the same as he responded. "He needs to watch where he's going," he said angrily, his gestures erratic with emotion.

"You need to watch where you're standing," Matty signed back dismissively. Matty had light brown skin and brown eyes with big, full eyelashes. His mom had been from Brazil originally, but she died when he was really young—years before he got turned into a werewolf and came to live with the Greers. He was almost a whole year younger than Charlie, but he was already half an inch taller, with long, gangly limbs and tightly curled brown-black hair that added a couple of extra inches. That meant he towered over Gideon, who was eight years old and short for his age.

"How does that make any sense?" Gideon snapped, his sharp, angry signs matching his tone. Gideon was round faced, with straight, silky black hair and warm brown skin. Unlike Matty and Opal, he wasn't technically an orphan, since he didn't really have parents—just a bunch of DNA from lots of people that had been combined to make a baby with special powers. Right now, those powers were making the air around him waver like a heat mirage. Charlie stepped up quickly.

"If you two get in a fight and make Mom and Dad miss their flight—" she started warningly, fixing Matty with a look.

They sprang apart guiltily. "I didn't do anything," Gideon muttered, pushing his glasses up and looking sullen.

"Not my fault I can't see him when he's so short," Mateo signed grumblingly, but Charlie put up a hand.

"You know how stressed Mom and Dad have been. This vacation has already been canceled three times because of us."

"Because of Matty," Gideon muttered.

"Because of *us*," Charlie repeated. "We have to convince them that we are totally on top of things and nothing will go wrong if they leave us alone, or they will cancel at the last second again and they will keep on getting more and more stressed until they pop like stressed-out balloons. Which means that we need to keep it together for another . . ." She checked her watch. "Twelve minutes. Can you do that? For Mom and Dad?"

They glared at each other. Matty's eyes flickered a brief, faint amber. Finally he signed a quick "fine" at her and turned on his heel, stomping down the stairs.

Gideon gave Charlie a plaintive look. "I didn't do anything," he said again.

She sighed and put a hand on his shoulder, giving it a squeeze. "You know how Matty gets this close to a full moon. Just hang in there." He made a little noise of understanding. At that moment her mother's voice called from downstairs.

"Charlie! Could you come here a minute?"

"I'll take care of the glass," Gideon said.

"You're sure?" Charlie asked.

"It's my fault it broke anyway. I lost control," he said, head hanging.

"I'm the one who was supposed to make sure those were secured better," Charlie pointed out, guilt twisting in her gut. Everything had to be earthquake-proof with a telekinetic eight-year-old in the house. She'd meant to get around to securing the pictures, she had, but there was always so much to do.

Charlie wasn't sure if Mateo was actually grumpy because of the full moon or because of preteen hormones. He sure had seemed grumpy most of the time lately, and when losing his temper meant shape-shifting into a four-legged menace to society, moodiness was a serious issue. Of course, they had to keep the furniture nailed down in case Gideon got upset, and when

Opal had nightmares, she almost burned the house down, so maybe Charlie shouldn't complain about Matty too much. Even if he always seemed to destroy *her* shoes when he went on a chewing spree.

Which was why Charlie puppy-proofed and earthquake-proofed and fireproofed the house and checked the fire extinguishers every week and made sure Gideon took his meds and that all their food was safe for his allergies and that Opal was never alone for too long, and she had an app to track the phases of the moon just in case because somehow Matty always forgot.

Her mom called her name again. Charlie clattered down the stairs into the hall, where her mom was digging through her enormous purse and muttering feverishly. The door was open behind her, and through it Charlie could see Agent Pendleton and Agent Baxter helping her dad load the car with luggage.

"Could have sworn I had them. They were right here. In the zipper pocket, where I couldn't possibly forget—there you are," Charlie's mom said, looking up and beaming at Charlie. Mateo had stomped off into the kitchen. Probably for a snack. He always seemed to be eating, and he only ever got skinnier and taller. "Charlie, darling, you wouldn't have seen the passports, by any chance?" Mom asked.

Charlie winced. "You lost the passports?"

"No, no. Of course not. I just don't have them," her mom said in a bright tone, her English accent making her sound all the more chipper. Leigh Greer was a petite woman, her blond hair cut in a long bob, a pair of reading glasses dangling around her neck. People usually expected her to dress in flowy, drapey fabrics or wool skirts and high collars, depending on what they pictured when they heard the word *psychic*. Instead, she was in her usual brightly colored T-shirt—this one featuring a dough-nut with a halo and the words *I'm So Hole-y!*—and mom jeans, an unzipped hoodie hanging from her shoulders.

"Did you check your desk?" Charlie asked.

Her mother gave her a look. "Charlie, if I put it in my desk, it has been devoured by the black hole of chaos and entropy that has taken up lodging there and we are doomed before we begin. I know I had them in my purse. And my purse was right here all night."

"I found them," a small voice said from above them. Charlie looked up. Opal's head was sticking through the ceiling.

"Opal, you know the rules. Use the stairs when there are guests," Mom chided.

Opal floated downward. "Agent Pendleton and Agent Baxter aren't guests," she objected, alighting on her feet.

"I suppose there's an argument to be made for that, but the front door is wide open, and a little bit of discretion wouldn't go amiss," Mom said, wagging her head.

To all appearances, Opal was a normal six-year-old girl with blond hair, pale skin, and a delicate array of freckles across her nose. She'd even learned to change her appearance enough that she was wearing a flowery dress and leggings instead of her usual white nightgown. Though if you moved your head right, you could see a few little wisps of smoke in the air around her, and when she got tired, she could go a bit transparent.

"You said you found the passports," Charlie prompted.

"Miss Sinister has them," Opal said meekly. "Up in the attic."

"Miss Sinister has what now?" Charlie's dad asked, stepping in from outside. He was in casual mode—jeans and a black T-shirt. His dark brown hair was starting to get some gray in it, and there were deep lines at the corners of his eyes. There was a scar on his cheek and more under his shirt, souvenirs of his and Mom's work.

"I believe she has absconded with the passports," Mom said, giving him a chagrined look.

The sigh that seeped out of him was one of deep resignation. "This is why I keep saying we need to keep her contained at night. Get her a crate or something."

"I'm not putting her in a cage, Kyle," Charlie's mom said firmly.

"We could make it nice. Some newspaper, a blanket. We could even give her some of the kids' homework to shred, keep her occupied," he said, giving Mom his you-can't-resist-me smile.

Charlie rolled her eyes. "I'll get the passports," she said. She didn't exactly love dealing with Miss Sinister, but at least she wouldn't have to watch her parents flirting.

"Quickly," Dad reminded her, tapping his watch. "Seven minutes and we are out of here."

Charlie waved a hand in acknowledgment and trotted back up the stairs, then down the hall, past where Gideon was picking up the last of the glass, to the narrow door that led to the rickety stairs up to the attic. She scaled them with some trepidation. The attic was dark, and when she reached for the light switch, nothing happened. The only light came from a dingy window. The dust was thick, and Charlie's nose started itching immediately. "Miss Sinister?" she called. Something scuttled in the corner of the room. "Miss Sinister, is that you?"

She pulled her phone out of her pocket and turned on the flashlight, shining it toward the corner of the room. It was empty except for an antique rocking chair, the wood faded and splitting. Under the chair was something dark, like a crumpled pile of fabric.

The pile of fabric twitched and twisted, and a small, pale face glared out from under the chair. It belonged to a doll wearing an old-fashioned black dress and a white bonnet. Patchy gray yarn stuck out from under the bonnet like hair, and the face was crudely carved, with lines beside its mouth where its chin could move up and down. Its eyes glowed red in the flashlight beam. It uttered a horrible hiss, wooden mouth clacking.

Poking out from under the doll's dress were the missing passports.

"Miss Sinister!" Charlie said sternly. "Bad doll. No stealing."

CHAPTER 2

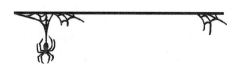

The doll hissed again, her tiny stiff hands shoving the passports more thoroughly under her layers of petticoats. Charlie strode over and reached under the chair, grabbing Miss Sinister firmly behind the head—the safest place to hold her if you didn't want to get bitten. She didn't have teeth, but she had a surprisingly strong jaw for something that was just connected with a bit of wire. Picking up the passports with her other hand, Charlie held the thrashing doll up to eye level.

"Why did you take Mom and Dad's passports?" Charlie asked her. "Are you trying to make them sad?"

The doll growled and swiped at her with a wooden hand, then crossed her arms and glared.

"You don't want Mom to leave, is that it?" Charlie asked. The doll didn't reply, setting her jaw and looking away. Charlie sighed. "They need this vacation, Miss Sinister. And they're not going to be gone very long. Just a week."

More grumpy silence. Charlie bent and set Miss Sinister on the ground gently, smoothing out her dress. "It'll be okay.

You can sleep in my bed, and I'll even pick you up some crickets from the pet store, okay?"

Miss Sinister perked up. Hunting crickets was one of the activities that brought her tiny cursed heart true joy. She wasn't exactly an *evil* doll. Just a *bad* one. As long as you kept her properly entertained, she didn't do much damage. Mom had gotten her in college after a sorority bought the doll from a flea market because they thought she was "quirky," not realizing she was cursed. After three months of terror, they'd been happy to let Mom collect her. Dad was always joking about getting rid of her, but sometimes Charlie caught him letting the doll sleep nestled in the crook of his arm like a teddy bear, and he'd been the one to buy her the giant cat tree in the living room.

Back in the entryway, Charlie brandished the passports.

"Thank you! Our hero." Mom beamed, gathering the passports and tucking them safely in her purse once again. "Is that everything?"

"Car's loaded up," Agent Baxter reported, stepping in from outside. He was white and a giant of a man, with a neck as wide as his jaw and a military precision to his stance. His husband, Agent Pendleton, slid in past him, maneuvering his much smaller body through the scant gap left in the hall. Pendleton was a short, slim Black man. He had high, sharp cheekbones and eyes that always looked a bit tired. Baxter and Pendleton were the junior agents in the DERI—the Division of Extranormal Research and Investigation. Charlie had known them her whole life.

Matty had come in from the kitchen, a smudge of peanut

butter on his lip. Gideon stood next to Charlie, and Opal hovered half an inch off the floor in front of them.

"Well then! I guess we should go," Mom said, and bit her lip. "Oh. Are you really going to be all right all by yourselves?"

"We're not all by ourselves, Mom," Charlie reassured her.

"Agent Baxter and Agent Pendleton can handle anything these kids throw at them," Dad said. He put a hand on Mom's shoulder. His tone was reassuring, but the look he cast at the two other agents said *or they'll have to answer to me.*

"Ms. Greer, your children will be safe with us. We will not let any harm come to them. You have my word," Baxter said gravely. Agent Baxter didn't know much ASL, but Gideon kept up a translation for Matty. "We are prepared for all threats, including boredom. I have *extensively* researched wholesome non-electronics-based modes of family entertainment and prepared several possible schedules to ensure an educational, engaging, and emotionally supportive experience across all six days, with contingencies in case of inclement weather. And I'm going to be making cookies. Lots of cookies, sir."

"I think she's more worried if we'll survive *them*," Agent Pendleton said, giving Charlie a wink. She flashed him a smile. She and Agent Pendleton had always gotten along. He was one of the few grown-ups she knew who talked to her like she was just a person who happened to be young, instead of a smaller, less intelligent version of an adult. Plus, he had an extensive collection of *Monster Monster Go!* cards and was always up for a quick battle.

"Uh-huh," Dad said, hands on his hips. "Then let's roll."

"Come here, my babies," Mom said, and opened her arms wide. Gideon stepped in for a hug right away, and she kissed the top of his head. Matty hung back, but she reached out and snagged him, pulling him in close, and even though he stiffened up like he didn't want a hug, Charlie saw him close his eyes and breathe in deep through his nose like he was memorizing her scent. Then he pulled away with an embarrassed groan and slouched over to the safety of the kitchen doorway.

Opal crept up, brow wrinkled in concentration. Mom put out her hands patiently and waited until Opal reached out. She pressed her palms gently against Mom's, focusing intently, and gave a little shiver of relief when they didn't pass through.

"Imagine the biggest, warmest hug," Mom said. "The very best hug ever. That's what I'm giving you right now."

"I'll miss you," Opal whispered.

"We'll be back before you know it," Dad promised. He knelt down to give Gideon a hug and went over to ruffle Matty's hair, which the lanky boy tolerated with a heaved sigh. "Charlie, want to give me a hand with this last bag?" he asked.

The last bag was just a small duffel, and he definitely didn't need help with it. But she nodded and walked out with him. He put a hand on her back as they walked and didn't say anything until they were out of easy earshot.

"Charlie, Pendleton and Baxter are in charge while we're gone. But I'm counting on you," he said, giving her a warm look.

"I know," Charlie said, scuffing her shoe against the driveway. "I'll make sure nobody gets into trouble."

He cuffed her shoulder affectionately. "I know that I can trust you to keep everybody safe. Right?"

"Right," Charlie said, lifting her eyes to his and tipping up her jaw. She *could* do this. Nobody knew her siblings like she did, or understood what they needed.

He rubbed his chin. "I don't know. Maybe this is the wrong time to be leaving. The full moon's in a few days. Opal's been phasing out again . . ."

"Dad, I've handled the full moon lots of times when you're traveling. And Opal's stressed because *you're* stressed," Charlie pointed out. "You've been working nonstop. Go have fun."

"You're right. Of course you're right, you're Charlie, and you're brilliant. Just remember—full moon Sunday night, so Matty needs to be in the basement before sunset. There's a new squeaky toy for him in the linen closet. Gideon should have plenty of meds, but make sure he takes them, and Pendleton's handling his ride to art class on Friday. Don't let Miss Sinister into the office while we're gone, and do not, under any circumstances, open the door to the Malice Vault. We'll be back next Tuesday. If anything goes wrong—"

"The emergency numbers are all on the fridge," Charlie finished for him. The emergency numbers were mostly for things like their doctor and dentist but also included contacts for specialists in cryptids, psychic disturbances, and interdimensional incursion. They'd come in handy a surprising number of times.

Charlie reached out and took her dad's hand, smiling her best I've-got-everything-under-control smile. "We're going to have a great time. Don't worry."

"What would I do without you, kiddo?" her dad asked, and squeezed her shoulder.

Mom bustled outside. "I haven't gotten my hug, Charlie," she said, and Charlie trotted over to supply it.

Along with her feelings, her knowings, and her hunches, Mom had the gift of the Soothe. It was how she could coax Opal into being a little girl instead of a ghost fading in and out of existence; it was how she had domesticated Miss Sinister and calmed the raging werewolf who had infected Matty. When she was around, curses got quieter, spells sang in harmony, and wicked spirits grew slow and sleepy.

It worked on normal people, too. When Leigh Greer put her hand on your shoulder, peace washed over you. It made her the best hugger in the country—and with Mom's arms wrapped around her, Charlie's worries melted away. Just for a moment.

Her mom smoothed back Charlie's coppery hair and pressed a kiss to her forehead. "Love you to infinity."

"And back," Charlie finished. She was going to miss her mom. Her parents traveled lots for their work, and it was hard to be apart every time. But her parents *needed* this. They needed a break from work and from home and from everything, needed it more than Charlie's siblings knew. More than Charlie was supposed to know. They had to go, and things had to be okay, and Charlie was going to make sure that nothing went wrong.

No matter what.

They parted. Hugs done. Bags packed. Two minutes to go. *They might actually make it to the car this time*, Charlie thought with mounting hope.

Mom opened the car door, then paused. "Oh, look. Agnes's house sold," she said, peering across the street.

Charlie followed her gaze. A moving truck sat in front of 1512 Oak Lane, still and silent. In thick, black letters on the side were the words MOVING TRUCK, as if there had been any confusion. The truck was perfectly ordinary, but something about it made the skin on the back of Charlie's neck prickle.

The house at 1512 had been empty for over a year, ever since Agnes Stanton and her sixteen cats had moved to Arizona. The bricks were crumbling, the roof had holes, and when you walked by at night, you could hear things scrabbling around under the house. Charlie's mom always called it a fixer-upper with potential. Charlie's dad called it a dump that would never sell. Then Charlie's mom would remind Charlie's dad that she was psychic and usually right about things, at which point Charlie's dad reminded Charlie's mom that she routinely lost her glasses when they were on top of her head, and then she would kiss him, and they would wander out of the room mooning at each other, and Charlie would bury her head in a book and pretend not to notice how annoyingly in love they were.

"Told you," Mom said, smirking at her husband.

"Those poor people don't know what they're in for," he said, shaking his head. Then he darted out a hand and snatched a file folder that had been sticking out of Mom's purse. She squawked in outrage, reaching for it, but he held it up out of her admittedly limited reach. "No bringing work with you," he scolded her.

"I'm onto something this time. I can feel it," Mom protested. "The White Elm case—"

"You're the one who's always calling *me* a workaholic. Charlie, take this inside and put it in the office, will you?"

"Aye, aye," Charlie said, retrieving it. It was thick with what looked like newspaper clippings and photographs. The label on the tab read THE ALMOST PEOPLE.

"Don't read that," her dad reminded her.

"I know the rules," she said, rolling her eyes. One minute to go. If they didn't get in the car now, they weren't going to make it.

Dad opened the driver's side. Mom opened the passenger side. They both got in and buckled their seat belts. Mom waved. From the porch, Matty, Gideon, Opal, and Agent Baxter waved back furiously. The car rolled into the street.

And they drove away.

Charlie's shoulders slumped with relief. They'd done it. Getting their parents to actually go on vacation was the hard part. Lasting the week without them should be easy by comparison.

Across the street at 1512 Oak Lane, the curtains twitched.

CHAPTER 3

Back inside, Baxter was already making good on his promise to bake cookies. He was wearing a floral apron and had his shirt cuffs rolled up to bare his impressively muscular arms as he toted bins of flour and sugar over to the counter, enlisting Matty to get out the eggs and milk. Even in his surliest moods, Matty could be bribed with the prospect of cookies. Pendleton had gotten out his *Monster Monster Go!* cards and was letting Gideon peruse his new acquisitions. Gideon wasn't as into the actual game as Charlie was, but he liked to look at the art. In the facility where he'd lived for the first four years of his life, he'd had nothing but plain gray walls. Now his room was covered in drawings and posters in every color of the rainbow.

That left Opal, who was sitting on the stairs with her chin in her hands. Tucking the file folder under her arm, Charlie went to sit next to her. "Everything okay?" she asked.

"I don't like it when people leave," Opal whispered. A wisp of smoke curled up from near her left shoulder.

Charlie gave her a reassuring smile. "They'll be back before you know it," she said. "It's Wednesday. They're coming back on Tuesday. One week, that's all."

Mom and Dad had found Opal haunting a house in San Francisco. It had been built on the site of a tenement house that had burned down in the 1920s. Three other houses had burned down in the same spot since, and half a dozen families in between had fled the constant phantom smoke smells, dreams of flickering flames, and the eerie, white-gowned girl who drifted through the halls at night. In the seventies a medium had even tried to exorcise Opal, but she'd driven him out. Mom was the first person who'd actually *talked* to Opal and realized how lost and confused she was. She didn't remember dying in that fire in 1926. All she remembered was that her family was suddenly gone, and every time she found a new one, they left her again.

Charlie wished that she could put an arm around Opal to comfort her. But it took a lot of effort for Opal to touch people or move objects. The best Charlie could do was sit with her and hope it was enough.

"What's that?" Opal asked, peering at the folder in Charlie's hands.

"Mom had it. I'm supposed to put it away. Want to come with me?" Charlie asked. Opal nodded—and, to Charlie's surprise, put out her hand. Charlie took it, watching the little furrowed line of concentration form between Opal's eyebrows. Her outline shimmered, her flowery dress turning back into a singed white nightgown, but her hand was solid as it slipped into Charlie's. Opal smiled in satisfaction. "You're getting so good at that," Charlie said, and the smile turned into a grin.

"I've been practicing lots," Opal chirped. Together, they walked up the stairs, and Opal's hand stayed solid the whole way. It had taken over a year of living with the Greers for her even to start existing most of the time, instead of popping in and out of awareness every few weeks. Another year for her to feel confident enough to start learning to control her appearance and intentionally manipulate physical objects. Charlie's heart filled with pride at how far Opal had come.

Mom and Dad's shared office was at the end of the hall. The door was locked, but instead of going for the key, Charlie winked at Opal and tilted her head toward the door. Opal darted through, and the lock turned from the other side. Charlie opened it and gave Opal a little round of applause. The blond ghost blushed and ducked her head.

Inside, the room was divided into Mom's side and Dad's side. Dad's side was orderly, with a big wooden desk and file folders. Mom's side was total chaos. Art she hadn't gotten around to hanging was leaned up against the wall, and there was a pile of discarded sweaters accumulating in her reading chair. She'd left her computer on her desk. The back was covered in colorful stickers, and there were about a million Post-it notes stuck all over the place near it. A pink one sticking to the lamp just said *REMEMBER TO DO THE THING.*

At the back of the room was a big, solid iron door. It had three dead bolts on it, along with a bunch of symbols in white paint. A keypad was mounted next to the door, the red light on it indicating that the system was locked.

Behind that door was the Malice Vault. In it was collected

some of the worst things that Charlie's parents had come across in all their years working for the Division of Extranormal Research and Investigation. Things that even the government couldn't contain. Without Mom and the Soothe around to help keep their energy at bay, their evil would grow and grow until it broke free. That was why she never went away for more than a couple of weeks, even for work.

There were about fifty layers of protections between the office and even the tamest of the Malices, but still Charlie kept her distance as she crossed to Mom's desk and left the file folder on top of it.

"Teddy bear filled with bugs," Opal said from the doorway.

Charlie shot her an amused look. It was a game they all played—making up things that *could* be in the Malice Vault. "Live bugs or dead ones?"

"Dead, but they come alive when you pick it up and crawl out all over you," Opal said, shuddering theatrically.

"Ewww," Charlie said appreciatively. "That's a good one."

"What do you think is actually in there, though?" Opal asked.

Charlie gave a casual shrug. "I don't know. Could be anything," she lied.

The truth was, she did know. She still had nightmares about the things in the Malice Vault. She'd wake up with her heart hammering, remembering the sound of the door slamming shut behind her and her mother screaming her name from the other side. She remembered the empty chair that wasn't empty at all. The small wooden box that whispered. The knife from which something dark and wet *drip, drip, dripped* in an endless rhythm. In her dreams, she wasn't alone. There was another girl there. A girl with red hair and bright blue eyes.

Let's be friends, the little girl said in her dreams, and every time she woke up screaming. Then Mom would be there, Soothing the nightmare away.

In the dreams, it felt like she'd been in the vault for a long, long time. But her parents said it had only been a few minutes before they rescued her.

Charlie glanced at the file on the desk again. *The Almost People*. Something about that name gave her the shivers. She was glad that Mom and Dad weren't working that case right now. She was proud of the work they did, but she was always worried, too. Sometimes it seemed like worrying was her only special ability, she did it so much.

For now, she reminded herself, the thing she had to worry about was making sure that everything ran smoothly while her parents were gone. Her phone chimed with a text message from her mom.

Leigh Greer (Mom)
10:26 a.m.

How's everything going?

You've only been gone five minutes!!! We're fine!!!

Everything was fine. And Charlie was determined to make sure it stayed that way for the next six days.

She left the office and closed the door firmly, and didn't notice the small bright-green spider that darted under the door and into the office behind her.

After dinner—Agent Baxter's famous pasta puttanesca—and the nightly chaos of getting everyone into bed, Charlie dragged herself to her bedroom and collapsed into the chair in front of her desk. Her phone was sitting out, lit up with notifications. Mom checking in (again) and a photo message. She checked it—a selfie of a bearded, intense-looking man dressed in all black with mirrored sunglasses, standing ominously in front of the Eiffel Tower. The phone chimed again as a text followed.

The Operative
7:23 p.m.

Doing some sightseeing after a job.
Picked you up some souvenirs

Are they weapons?

No
Well
Are knives weapons

YES.

Okay yes they're weapons.

Dad told you to stop buying us weapons.
No explosives either.

What about explosives?
Oh sorry I was already typing.
Okay but then I'm out of ideas.

How about a T-shirt.

Huh.
I never would have thought of that.

That concerns me.

Charlie let out a sigh and rubbed her forehead. Mom and Dad's work friends were nice and all—well, sort of—but they had a tendency to complicate situations. And occasionally overthrow governments. She made a mental note to see if there was any weird, inexplicable news coming out of Paris. Or maybe she didn't want to know.

She started typing again.

You got that doll for Opal for her birthday,
remember?
That was good. That was progress.
Think dolls, NOT explosives.

Right. The doll. The doll that is not an explosive.

The not-explosive doll.
That doll.

Charlie's eyebrows shot up.

Do I need to be worried about the doll.

Hey so I heard your folks are taking a trip.
Let me know if you need anything.

EVERYTHING IS FINE PLEASE DON'T HELP

Right-o
👍

Just then, Charlie's door creaked open behind her, and a familiar scuttling sound raced across the floor. By the time she turned around, all she could see was the open door and a lump under her covers. She sighed and stood up, walking over to the bed. "Miss Sinister," she said. The lump shook a bit and growled. "Miss Sinister, get out from under the covers."

The doll hunkered down. Charlie peeled back the blankets, revealing the huddled doll, who clacked her wooden mouth threateningly.

"You can stay in my room, but only if you don't attack my feet," Charlie said. The doll creaked out a sound that might have been agreement. Charlie could never tell just how much language she understood. She seemed about as intelligent as a dog or a cat most of the time, but it was hard to say for sure.

Movement outside the window caught Charlie's eye. There was someone standing on the lawn of 1512. Three some-ones, actually: a man, a woman, and a boy who looked about Charlie's age. They were standing together, the parents behind the child. All of them were looking across the street at Charlie's house. And all of them were smiling.

There was something very strange about the way the light from the streetlamps hit their eyes. It was like they were reflec-tive, shining with a flat, eerie white. Their smiles were perfect and stiff, and Charlie checked to see if there was someone else taking their picture—they seemed like they were posing. But they were alone out there. Charlie stared, waiting for them to move or for their smiles to fade, but they just stood there. Smiling. Charlie shivered, not entirely sure why it was so unsettling.

Miss Sinister shot across the bed in a flurry of movement, pouncing on something on the windowsill and startling Charlie, who gave a squeak. The doll looked up, three bright-green, spider-like legs sticking out of her mouth. She growled, clacked her jaw to chew the spider up, and swallowed.

Where the things she ate went, no one knew. And Charlie wasn't about to investigate.

"Gross," she told the doll, who scampered off the end of the bed and clambered into Charlie's desk chair, where she crouched lumpishly. Charlie glanced back out the window. The neighbors were gone. Weird. But then, she couldn't exactly throw stones—her family would always be the weirdest one on the block.

Still, she stood there frowning at 1512 for several minutes before she dragged herself to bed.

CHAPTER 4

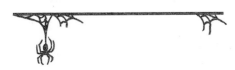

The next morning, Charlie came downstairs to discover Gideon and Opal already up, sitting at the kitchen table with heaps of pancakes slathered in syrup and piled high with blueberries in front of them. Opal had her eyes shut and her nose hovering half an inch above her stack, smiling blissfully, while Gideon shoveled in mouthfuls.

"Morning, Miss Charlotte," Baxter said, expertly flipping a pancake the size of her head. "I hope you're hungry."

"Starved," Charlie confirmed.

Pendleton was rooting through the cupboards. "Don't your parents have any coffee?" he asked. He scratched the back of his neck, itching at a red bump.

"Just tea," Charlie said.

Pendleton gave her a baleful look. "That's just unnatural," he muttered, closing the cupboards in defeat.

"Have a pancake. It'll make everything better," Baxter said, holding out a plate. Pendleton took it with a look that said it did not, in fact, make everything better, but he wasn't going to turn down free pancakes. Right then, Matty came thumping down the steps, still half asleep, and oozed into the seat next to Opal. Soon they were all chowing down on pancakes.

"Looks like your new neighbors are moving in," Pendleton said, nodding toward the kitchen window. Sure enough, the family Charlie had seen last night was walking between the moving truck and the house, carrying cardboard boxes.

"There's a kid your age, Charlie," Baxter said. "Could be your new best friend just moved in."

"I've already got friends," Charlie muttered, dragging a bite through a puddle of syrup. It wasn't exactly true. There were people she was friendly with at school, but the existence of were-wolves and ghosts and kids with powers wasn't widely known. When you had to explain why your sister couldn't go to the park because she hadn't learned to exist outside a 500-foot radius of her house to someone who didn't even believe in ghosts, things got awkward fast. Besides, she didn't have time for hanging out and going to movies, or whatever kids her age were supposed to do. She had to be home to take care of her siblings.

Gideon reached for the blueberries, and Charlie frowned at the big red bump on the back of his hand. "What happened there?" she asked.

He looked down at it and shrugged. "Something bit me, I guess. No biggie."

Charlie sighed. "I'll get the first aid kit."

"You don't have to," Gideon protested, but she was already getting up. Gideon wasn't good at taking care of himself. Or letting other people take care of him. Their parents had rescued him from a super sketchy experimental facility where they were trying to develop his telekinetic powers into a weapon. He hadn't even known what a teddy bear was when Mom and Dad first brought him home.

As she was putting ointment on the bite and bandaging it up, Baxter cleaned up the plates.

"We should head over there. Give them a hand. Bring some cookies," he said. "It's the neighborly thing to do. Do you think they like nuts? Could have food allergies. What if they're vegans? I'm going to have to make more cookies."

"Why don't we ask them, and you can make the perfect cookies later," Pendleton said. He ducked his head and said in a quiet voice to Charlie, "If you don't stop him at this point, you end up with eight dozen cookies and no flour left in a three-state radius." Charlie stifled a laugh.

"Good call," Baxter acknowledged. With military efficiency, he rinsed and stacked the plates and dried his hands on his apron. "All right, troops. Shoes on. It's time to introduce yourselves."

Charlie thought of the way the neighbors had just *stood* there last night. Something about them made her uneasy.

No. *Not* uneasy. Because if they made her feel uneasy, there might be something wrong. And if there was something wrong, Mom and Dad would come home, and they wouldn't get their vacation, and then . . .

She didn't want to think about that.

They were just the new neighbors. Probably perfectly friendly and very normal. She fixed a smile on her face. "I'd love to," she said.

"Excellent!" Baxter said. He clapped his hands together. "Well, then. Hop to it, buckaroos!"

Pendleton heaved himself to his feet, settling his tie. "I have to go into the office. You all have fun carrying boxes without me," he said, and with a two-fingered salute ambled to the door.

Charlie looked at her siblings. Gideon was already pulling his shoes on. He pretty much always did what he was told, especially when instructions came from someone with authority. Mom was always urging him to rebel at least a little, but it was hard for him after the way he'd spent his first few years. Matty, on the other hand, was slumped against the wall, clearly uninterested. If anything, Matty had the opposite problem—he hated following instructions. He'd been in a bunch of different foster homes before he got turned into a werewolf. Then he'd spent a few weeks surviving all by himself as a stray puppy before Mom and Dad found him. He was used to doing things all on his own.

"I don't want to go," Opal confessed in a whisper, and Charlie startled. She hadn't seen Opal hovering at her elbow, which was probably because she was mostly transparent. They couldn't exactly keep their neighbors from knowing there was something strange about their family, but none of them knew *how* strange. And people had a way of not noticing things that didn't make sense—like the fact that Opal hadn't aged at all in the last five years. Somehow, they all just ignored that the rest of the kids were growing up and Opal was getting further and further behind.

Charlie looked over at Baxter. "Agent Baxter? Opal's not

feeling solid enough for new people," Charlie said. Opal gave her a grateful look.

"Are you sure that you're not depriving yourself of the opportunity for rewarding social encounters because of anxiety?" Baxter asked. He crouched down to be eye level with Opal. "You will meet your new neighbors eventually. Maybe it's better to do it when everybody's getting introduced at once, so you don't have to feel like the center of attention. We can look out for you, and you can pop back here whenever you need to."

Opal bit her lip. Slowly, she grew more solid and gave a tiny nod. Charlie regarded Baxter with a newly impressed look. He'd actually had a very good point. Interacting with the outside world was hard for Opal, but it was also important—it kept her real.

"Fantastic," Baxter said, standing up. He looked at Matty. "I don't see any shoes on those feet."

"Do I have to go?" Matty asked.

"Everyone else is going," Charlie pointed out. "Come on, Mr. Lone Wolf. It'll make Baxter happy."

Matty rolled his eyes but trudged over to his shoes. He shoved them on without untying them and headed out after Baxter. Charlie stopped to lace hers up properly, and by the time she got outside, Baxter and the others were already across the street. Baxter was introducing himself to the new neighbors and gesturing broadly back at the house.

The man and the woman she'd seen last night stood shoulder to shoulder in front of Baxter, smiling identical smiles. As she approached, their eyes ticked over to her at the exact same time, an effect so startling, she almost stumbled. Both of them were white with medium-brown hair. The man's was parted on the side and swept across his brow. He wore thick black glasses and a green sweater-vest above khaki slacks. The woman wore a black-and-white polka-dot sundress and kitten heels.

"And this is Charlotte Greer. A.k.a. Charlie. Her skills include lacrosse and *Monster Monster Go!*" Baxter said, as if delivering a briefing to his superiors. Charlie spread her fingers in a half-hearted wave.

"It's very nice to meet you, Charlie. I am Mr. Weaver," the man said, extending a hand. Charlie shook it. His skin was cool and smooth. He was wearing a name tag sticker, she noticed, but instead of just his name, he'd written THIS IS MR. WEAVER. His handwriting was scratchy, like he'd gone over it several times.

"And I am Mrs. Weaver," the woman said, which Charlie already knew since she was also wearing a name tag that read THIS IS MRS. WEAVER in the same handwriting. She put out her own hand. It was exactly the same texture and exactly the same temperature as her husband's. Charlie suppressed a shiver. She was just being paranoid, she told herself—used to seeing strange things everywhere because of what her family did for a living.

"And this is our darling son, Peter," Mrs. Weaver said, flourishing a hand to indicate the boy, who was walking back across the front lawn. Peter was dressed just like his father, though his sandy-brown hair was a little bit shaggy, and his button-up shirt had come untucked from his belt. He had a name tag, too. Did people usually wear name tags when they moved into a new neighborhood?

"Hello. It's nice to meet you," Peter said politely, but didn't put out his hand.

"Thought you might need some help with these boxes. Is it just the three of you?" Baxter asked, eyeing the large moving truck with some surprise.

"We decided to save the expense of hiring movers," Mr. Weaver said, smiling. "A little bit of hard work never hurt anyone. Isn't that right, Mrs. Weaver?"

"Absolutely, Mr. Weaver," she gushed.

"Well, let me haul a few boxes for you at least," Baxter said.

"Oh, we wouldn't want to trouble you," Mrs. Weaver said.

"It's no trouble at all. Plus I've got my trusty assistants here," Baxter said.

"If you're certain it's not a bother," Mrs. Weaver said. It was remarkable, Charlie thought, how she managed to speak without her smile ever slipping. Baxter seemed entirely charmed—and so, to Charlie's surprise, did Gideon and Matty. Gideon she could understand, but Matty? He was smiling dopily as he marched off to the back of the moving truck to grab a box. Opal, of course, hung back, but Gideon was right on Matty's heels. Mr. Weaver and Baxter followed after, leaving Mrs. Weaver and Peter to beam at Charlie and Opal.

"Let's let the boys handle the heavy lifting. You ladies can stay here with me," Mrs. Weaver said.

"I can help," Charlie said, rankled at the suggestion that she wouldn't want to because she was a girl. "Don't go anywhere, Opal."

Peter was watching Charlie with a sharp expression that

didn't match his smile, and when she set off after the boys, he tagged along.

"Your siblings don't really look like you," he said.

She gave him a skeptical look. "Never heard of adoption?"

"I was just curious," he replied. He cleared his throat. "It's cool that there are kids in the neighborhood. I was worried I wouldn't have any friends." The line sounded rehearsed.

"There are plenty of kids in the neighborhood," Charlie said.

"Maybe you could introduce me," he replied as they reached the back of the truck. Baxter lumbered by, struggling under a large box labeled HEAVY. Matty and Gideon trailed behind with smaller loads.

"I don't think that would be a good idea, if you want friends," Charlie said, shaking her head.

"Why not?"

"They don't like me, that's why not," Charlie snapped, not looking at him. She grabbed a box that was sitting out on the ground. It was labeled DISHES, and she'd expected it to have some heft, but when she lifted it, she nearly threw it by accident. It was light as a feather—practically empty. *Must be mislabeled dish towels or something*, she thought, and stacked it on top of another box. She lifted both of them—and the weight hardly seemed different. "What's in these, anyway?" she asked.

"Sundries," Mr. Weaver said, appearing in front of her. He reached out and took hold of the boxes. "I'll get those. Don't trouble yourself."

"I can carry them," Charlie insisted, but Mr. Weaver was already lifting them out of her grasp. She picked up another box, more gingerly this time, and it was just as light as the others—and just as quickly taken from her hands, this time by Peter.

Dish towels, she thought. *Napkins. A collection of papier-mâché sculptures.* There were lots of reasons for none of the boxes to weigh anything—right?

She picked up a fourth featherlight box and marched quickly toward the house. She'd gotten nearly to the front door when Mr. Weaver stepped through and reached for her load.

"You're so very helpful," he said. "I'll take it from here."

"I've got it," she assured him, keeping her grip.

His smile didn't falter, and he didn't move. It was like Mr. Weaver didn't want her to go inside—but he'd been fine with letting the boys in, and now Matty and Agent Baxter were stepping out as if nothing was wrong. Charlie craned her neck to try to see in the door, but it swung shut before she could catch a glimpse of anything more than the nondescript, if slightly dusty, entryway.

"I think your brother is feeling unwell. Maybe you should walk him home," Mr. Weaver said.

"What?" Charlie asked, alarmed.

At that moment, Gideon emerged from the house. He looked a little dazed. "I have a headache," he said, blinking at her. "Can you walk me home?"

Charlie looked between the smiling Mr. Weaver and Gideon, and back again suspiciously.

"I really don't feel good," Gideon said. His face was flushed.

Charlie gave up her grip on the box. She waved Gideon toward her. "Come on. I'll get you home."

He wobbled over to her, and she put an arm around him as she walked him down toward the street, casting one last suspicious glance behind her. Matty returned to the moving truck and grunted as if with effort as he lifted another box—but it seemed weirdly like an act. The box didn't sit heavily enough in his arms to match the expression of effort on his face. Charlie pressed her lips together in a tight line.

She was letting her anxious imagination run wild. There was nothing weird happening at 1512, she told herself.

Mrs. Weaver was still out at the curb, chatting with Opal. As soon as Charlie and Gideon got close, Opal hurried over to join them.

"Leaving so soon?" Mrs. Weaver asked. Charlie muttered something about Gideon's headache and picked up her pace.

Inside the house, Charlie put her hand to Gideon's forehead. "You feel cold. How bad is your head?"

"Not great," he said. He looked a bit gray. He got a lot of headaches, but this must be a bad one. She winced sympathetically.

"Why don't you go up to bed. I'll bring you the ice pack and some meds," she promised him, keeping her voice soft. He nodded miserably and started toward the stairs.

"Gideon?" she asked, trying and failing to ignore the uneasy feeling scratching away at the base of her skull. He paused at the bottom of the stairs. "Did your headache start when you were in the house? Did something happen in there?"

"It was just a nice, normal house," Gideon said, sounding confused.

"Okay. That's good. I'll be right up," Charlie said, relaxing a bit. Gideon was prone to headaches. He always had been. It was just a coincidence. She headed into the kitchen to grab the ice pack, Opal trailing behind.

"What were you talking about with Mrs. Weaver?" she asked Opal, telling herself it was just curiosity.

"Normal stuff," Opal said, but she made a face. "She never stopped smiling. And she kept asking me questions that were normal, but weird, too? Like, 'What activities do you enjoy? What television programs do you watch?' She kept saying them the same way. I don't know. I didn't like it."

"None of them ever stopped smiling," Charlie said, very much *not* smiling herself. She bit her lip. "You don't think . . . there isn't something weird about them, is there?"

"Because they're too friendly?" Opal asked curiously.

It wasn't exactly compelling evidence. She imagined writing up a report for the Division. New neighbors moved into a suburban neighborhood in Virginia. Upon arrival, they displayed excessive cheer and inquired about resident six-year-old's leisure activities in a condescending manner. Neighbors were promptly apprehended and jailed for all eternity.

"Should we call Mom and Dad?" Opal asked, a hint of hopefulness in her voice.

"Absolutely not," Charlie said immediately. Opal deflated. "We can't interrupt them. No matter what. Right?"

Opal nodded glumly. "Right."

"Five more days," Charlie told her. They could make it five days.

She thought of Mom with her head in her hands, Dad with his hand on her back. Mom's quavering voice. *I don't know how much longer I can do this.*

Mom and Dad needed this. Which meant they needed *her* to make sure that everything at home was taken care of. And that's what Charlie was good at. That's what made Charlie special—taking care of people like Mom and Opal and Matty and Gideon.

She wasn't going to let them down.

CHAPTER 5

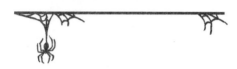

Matty and Agent Baxter came home full of energy. "Mrs. Weaver gave us fresh homemade lemonade," Matty said as he slung himself onto the couch, his long limbs splayed over every available inch. "It was so good."

Charlie, who was curled up in an armchair with a book, gave him a skeptical look. Without any of his siblings over there, Matty would have only had Agent Baxter to translate for him, and Baxter's vocabulary was pretty limited. Usually, being left out of conversations made Matty surly. Instead, he was the most cheerful she'd seen him in months.

"They're such a charming family," Baxter declared, hands on his hips. "And no food allergies. I think I'll go with snicker-doodles. Or caramel pecan. Or both. Definitely both."

Matty turned on the television and pressed play on a recording of a soccer match—football, Matty would correct her. He was totally obsessed with the Brazil national football team and had posters of them all over his room. He'd gotten Dad into it, too, even if Dad occasionally pretended to argue that American football was better, just to tease him.

Charlie waved a hand to get Matty's attention. "What was the inside like?" she signed. "It looked dusty."

"It's not that bad," he answered. "They need to do some cleaning up. But it was very nice. A nice, normal living room. And Mrs. Weaver made us a pitcher of fresh homemade lemonade."

"You mentioned," Charlie replied, rolling her eyes. The way to Matty's heart was definitely his stomach. "What else did you see?"

Matty waved a hand in annoyance. "Go see it yourself if you're that interested."

"Maybe I will," she said, but he had already turned his attention back to the TV and didn't see.

Throughout the rest of the day, Charlie kept glancing out the window. The Weavers unloaded box after box. They must be leaving the heavy stuff for last—or maybe they'd already brought it in? She didn't remember seeing any furniture in the truck, but maybe it had been hidden behind the boxes.

Gideon was still in bed hours later. The meds had helped with his headache, but he looked tired and pale, and when she checked on him, he was curled up on his side holding Timothy, his stuffed elephant, tight against his chest. He didn't do that much anymore.

She sat on the edge of the bed. "Hey, Timothy. How's your best buddy doing?" she asked the elephant.

Timothy's ears wiggled almost imperceptibly, moved by Gideon's powers. "Not so good," Gideon said weakly in his Timothy voice, which sounded suspiciously like Agent Baxter.

"Do you think you're coming down with something?" she asked.

"I don't know. I feel like . . . like a jar of peanut butter when you're trying to scrape out the last bits," Gideon said. He buried his nose in Timothy's soft head.

"Just rest," Charlie said. "I'm sure you'll feel better in the morning."

Gideon nodded and snuggled deeper under the covers.

Charlie left the room frowning. He'd gotten sick after he went into the Weavers' house. But Matty and Baxter were fine, so that had to be a coincidence.

By evening, Charlie had just about convinced herself that she was imagining things. She was jumping at shadows, that was all.

When she went to bed, there was a text from Dad.

Kyle Greer (Dad)
9:12 p.m.

House still standing?

We're fine.

You're fine AND
you haven't burned
down the house?

Not yet. We're doing that tomorrow.

Ha ha. Are you looking after your siblings?

Of course. Everyone's good.

Baxter mentioned Gideon wasn't feeling well.

Charlie winced. She should have guessed that the agents would be providing detailed updates. Anything Baxter and Pendleton knew, her parents would find out right away.

He's a little sick. Just resting. Don't worry, I can look out for him.

She hesitated, fingers hovering over the screen for a moment before she typed again.

By the way, we met the new neighbors.

What are they like?

They're nice.

She stared at the last text, willing herself to believe it. Her dad sent her a couple more messages, just saying he loved her and he'd see her soon.

Nice, normal texts, she thought, and for some reason the words made her skin crawl.

She sat up reading late into the night, watching through the gap in her curtains, but the Weavers didn't come outside again.

CHAPTER 6

Gideon was feeling well enough the next morning to come downstairs for homemade waffles. He had circles under his eyes and Timothy clamped under one arm, but he was cheerful enough as Baxter poured on extra syrup to "get his energy back up." Charlie hid her relief—and rescued Timothy from a sticky fate, swooping him off the table just before Gideon got too enthusiastic about his breakfast.

"You owe me a *Monster Monster Go!* rematch today," Pendleton reminded her. He'd brought a french press and a bag of coffee from work and was watching her over the rim of his mug, leaning against the counter. Baxter, manning the waffle iron, had his earbuds in, occasionally busting out off-key Taylor Swift lyrics.

"I'll just stomp you again," Charlie said to Pendleton with a raised eyebrow.

"I don't know. I think I'll surprise you," Pendleton replied.

"Not if you stick with that Beast/Mystic deck," Charlie said. "You've been trying to make that work for like two years."

"Beast/Mystic has the coolest pictures," Gideon piped up from the table.

Charlie looked upward in despair. "You can't just pick based on the *pictures*. You need strategy," she said.

"I dunno, I think it's about the cool pictures," Pendleton said, goading her good-naturedly. He scratched idly at his upper arm. "What do you think, Gideon? Want to help me make a new deck to trounce your sister with?"

"Yeah!" Gideon said, brandishing a syrup-coated fork.

At that moment, the doorbell rang. "I'll get it," Charlie offered.

She could see the distinctive silhouette of Mrs. Weaver in her A-line dress through the frosted windows next to the door. When she opened the door, she realized Peter was there as well, standing at the edge of the porch steps with his hands in his pockets, his shoulders slouched. Mrs. Weaver beamed. She was wearing a dress that was almost exactly the same as the day before, except that it was reversed—black with white polka dots, instead of the other way around, but still with a bright red belt at her waist. She and Peter were both still wearing their name tags—or maybe new name tags. There was a small gray hoodie draped over Mrs. Weaver's thin arm.

"Good morning, Miss Greer," Mrs. Weaver said. "Your darling brother left his jacket at our house. We thought we might return it." She rested a hand on the hoodie.

"Thanks," Charlie said politely, and reached for it.

"I thought I might give it back to him directly and see how

he's doing," Mrs. Weaver said. "We've been ever so worried about him."

Charlie stared at her. *Neighborly concern*, she thought. *It's just neighborly concern.*

"My jacket!" Gideon had appeared behind her and now scurried forward enthusiastically. "Thanks, Mrs. Weaver." He stepped up beside Charlie and reached for the hoodie. Instead of just handing it to him, Mrs. Weaver bent down and held it out for him to slip on, smiling indulgently. Gideon was happy enough to let her. Even in the summer heat, he liked wearing jackets and cozy socks.

"What a delightful little dumpling you are," Mrs. Weaver said. She smoothed the front of the hoodie and tucked his hair back from his face. Her fingertip brushed lightly across his forehead, and Charlie almost thought she saw a faint glimmer of light where the tip of her finger touched his skin. Just for a moment. And maybe she hadn't seen it at all. But Charlie narrowed her eyes.

"Mom. We should get back," Peter said. Mrs. Weaver straightened up abruptly. There were points of bright pink on her cheeks.

"Back. Yes. So many preparations to make," she said, folding her hands in front of her.

"Preparations?" Charlie asked. She pulled Gideon back against her, putting an arm over his chest and trying not to look *too* protective. What had that been? Just a trick of the light?

"Unpacking," Peter said.

"Right," Charlie said slowly.

"Have a wonderful day, children," Mrs. Weaver said. She turned away, stepping primly down from the porch. Peter lingered a moment, looking back at Charlie. It was almost like he wanted to say something more. But then Mrs. Weaver called his name, and he trudged after her.

Charlie shut the door behind them and looked down at Gideon. His eyes were unfocused, and he looked a bit pale. "Hey. You okay?" she asked him.

He put a hand to his stomach. "I think I ate too much waffle," he said.

"You feel sick?"

He nodded glumly. "I think I better go back to bed," he said.

Charlie sank down into a crouch and looked up into his face, putting a hand to his forehead. He felt cool to the touch, almost clammy. Like he had when he'd come out of the Weavers' house.

"Go lie down," she told him. "I'll bring you some tea."

It was probably just some little bug.

But what if it wasn't?

Charlie watched the Weavers' house from her window. They hadn't come out again. There was no movement at all.

Gideon was sick. Again. Admittedly, that was hardly new for him. He was fragile, and he'd grown up in a sealed lab, so his immune system wasn't exactly robust. Sometimes it seemed like he could catch a cold just by thinking about it.

But still, it bothered her—the Weavers being there both

times he felt sick, and that glimmer of light when Mrs. Weaver had touched him.

She chewed her lip. Was she being paranoid?

She hoped she was. She wanted to be wrong. But she couldn't ignore something that might be putting her siblings in danger.

She had to get a look inside that house.

A few minutes later, Charlie marched into the kitchen as Baxter was rummaging in the cupboards, muttering about pecans.

"Agent Baxter?"

"Yes, Miss Charlotte?" he asked. If anyone else called her that she'd be annoyed, but everything Agent Baxter did was both extremely polite and completely genuine. Agent Pendleton sometimes teased him about it, but she knew it was part of why Agent Pendleton loved him in the first place. Pendleton had been assigned to the Division to spy on her parents. Eventually he'd ended up on their side instead, but it meant he'd spent a lot of time lying and keeping secrets. Baxter was all about honesty and openness, and when your whole life was once about shadows and betrayal, someone you could take at their word and rely on completely was pretty amazing.

"I was thinking I could help you make the cookies. Then I could deliver them to the Weavers for you," Charlie said brightly. She should leave it alone, she knew. And she would. Just as soon as she saw inside the house and reassured herself that there was nothing suspicious going on.

Baxter straightened up, the bag of pecans in his hand, and looked down at her. "I know what you're doing," he said.

She blinked. "What I'm doing?" she squeaked.

"You're sad you missed out on the lemonade. Hoping to get a taste for yourself, are you?" he said, and chuckled.

She gave a relieved smile. "Yeah. You found me out," she said, snapping her fingers.

"Your secret's safe with me," he said, giving an exaggerated wink. "Now grab an apron and let's get baking."

"Yes, sir," she said. In her pocket, her phone chimed. She checked it quickly as Baxter went to the fridge for the eggs. It was a text. The contact hadn't been in her phone a few minutes ago—and she hadn't created it. It was Director Winter. Director Winter was the head of A.D.E.P.T.—a shadowy secret organization sworn to "Acquire, Defend against, and Eliminate Paranormal Threats" (which Charlie thought was kind of an awkward acronym, though she'd never tell the director that). She was also Charlie's godmother.

Director Winter—A.D.E.P.T.

8:13 a.m.

> I hear you've been
> left in charge.
> A great responsibility.

I'm not in charge!
Agent Baxter and Agent Pendleton
are babysitting.

>   Baxter is a fool. Pendleton is a cog in a machine
>   he does not understand. But you are up to the
>   task.

Um, thanks?

>   Do not mistake my words for idle praise.
>   I have no patience for flattery.
>   I merely offer my assessment of your capabilities.

Well, if I need anything, I'll be sure to give you a
call.
Just kidding, legally you don't exist, I've never
heard of you, etc.

>   Good girl.

The contact deleted itself from her phone, along with all the messages. Charlie sighed and grabbed her apron. First the Operative, and now Director Winter? Did everyone in the world know their parents were on vacation? It was hardly the first time their parents had traveled, but they hadn't been gone at the same time for more than a couple of days in a row since adopting Matty. The Operative and Director Winter were probably just being a little overprotective, which made a certain amount of sense, given that their lives involved an unusual degree of deadly peril.

Being the child of Kyle and Leigh Greer hadn't exactly been

normal even before her siblings arrived. There were all the business trips, the injuries, the coming home with monster goo in their hair, the discussions cut short at the dinner table when they remembered that anything involving the words *rampaging shark-bear hybrid* probably wasn't suitable for a five-year-old. Mom and Dad had both been abducted multiple times, and even Charlie had gotten kidnapped once, along with Agent Pendleton. Luckily, they'd just been locked in an old cabin by a cult who thought that Mom could open a portal to a realm of demons that turned out not to exist. They'd mostly spent the time playing Crazy Eights and one very long game of Monopoly.

That was why they hadn't gone on a real vacation in years. They didn't want to leave their kids unprotected if there was any kind of threat. But things had been calm for the last couple of years, and Charlie and her siblings were old enough to mostly look after themselves.

And things were still calm, Charlie told herself. The Weavers were pleasant people. She was being paranoid, and it was nothing to bother Mom and Dad about. She would go over there, and she would see that everything was fine, and Mom and Dad wouldn't have to worry.

As soon as the cookies had cooled, Baxter piled them on a plate, and Charlie carried them across the street, striding with purpose. She stepped up onto the porch, and reached out to ring the bell.

Nothing happened. It must be broken. She reached out and knocked sharply instead, then waited.

She listened for footsteps, but there were none. She was about to turn and go, figuring they'd left without her noticing, when the door popped open. She jumped, surprised, and nearly dropped the plate.

"Oh dear. Didn't mean to startle you," Mr. Weaver said, smiling.

She tried to mirror his smile. "That's all right. I didn't hear you coming, that's all," she said. Which seemed a little strange, didn't it? The hallway was tile, and Mr. Weaver was wearing loafers. She should have heard footsteps.

"I'm light on my feet," Mr. Weaver said, chuckling like this was a fantastic joke. "What can I do for you, Miss Greer?"

Baxter's *Miss Charlotte* had been charming. *Miss Greer* made her clamp her back teeth together, and she wasn't sure why. "I brought you some cookies," she said.

"Wonderful. How neighborly of you," Mr. Weaver said, reaching out. But she kept the plate close to her chest.

"I thought I could bring them inside for you," she said.

"Oh, I'm afraid we aren't up for company right now," Mr. Weaver replied.

"The thing is, I heard about Mrs. Weaver's amazing lemonade," Charlie said. She tried to lean as casually as she could to see past Mr. Weaver's shoulder, but he was blocking her view quite effectively.

"Agent Baxter and your brother drank it all," Mr. Weaver said, and this time when he reached out, Charlie couldn't keep the plate away from him without actually yanking it out of his hands—so she let go. "Thank you so much. I'm sure we'll find time to have you over soon," he said, and shut the door without another word.

Charlie stood blinking at the door for a moment. Movement at the edge of her vision caught her eye, and she turned her head to see a small bright-green spider descending a line of silk from the awning, heading straight toward her left shoulder.

"Whoops," she said, stepping neatly out of the way. She wasn't a fan of spiders, but she didn't have Miss Sinister's murderous inclination toward them. As long as they didn't bother her, she left them alone. This one waved its tiny legs at her, almost as if it was mad she'd gotten away. "I think I'm a bit too big for a snack," she told it. Then, sighing, she plodded her way back across the street.

She hadn't gotten a glimpse inside. It really did seem like Mr. Weaver didn't want her going in there. They hadn't invited Opal in, either. Why?

The Greers' next-door neighbors, the Crispin-Suzukis, were getting out of their van when Charlie reached the other side of the street. Ms. Suzuki gave Charlie a distracted little wave, then peered intently at her phone. She was a short, intense woman with a very important job that Charlie only knew had something to do with finance. Her twin daughters, Juliana and Melody, went to Charlie's school.

"Good morning, Charlie," Mr. Crispin said, getting out of the driver's side. He was a big guy with a prominent belly and un-usually bushy eyebrows. He used to run a catering company, but it had gone out of business during the pandemic, and he'd decided to be a "house spouse" instead. He had a huge garden in the back, and the lawn out front was immaculate—which he kept that way by mowing right outside Charlie's bedroom window every Saturday at 7:00 a.m.

"Morning, Mr. Crispin," she said. She took a step toward her house, but he kept talking.

"Saying hello to the new neighbors, were you?" he asked.

"Dropping off some cookies," she explained.

He scratched the back of his neck. "What do you think of them?" he asked.

Juliana, tapping away at her own phone, heaved a sigh. "Da-ad. They're a perfectly nice, normal family." Privately, Charlie thought it was unlikely Juliana would notice if they were twelve-foot-tall fire-breathing lizard monsters, given how rarely she looked up from her phone.

"Who's that?" Ms. Suzuki asked.

"The new neighbors. The ones I was telling you are a little strange," Mr. Crispin said, and Charlie's eyebrows shot up. So she wasn't the only one who'd noticed.

"They didn't seem that strange to me," Melody said, but there was a puzzled little frown tugging at the corners of her mouth. Melody and Charlie had almost been friends. They'd been on the lacrosse team together. Charlie had loved lacrosse. And she'd really liked spending time with Melody. But two weeks in, Opal had a panic attack, and Charlie wasn't there to help. Matty did his best to calm her down, but she lit the curtains on fire, and Gideon couldn't remember how to use the fire extinguisher, and it was very nearly a complete disaster. And lacrosse was two hours three days a week and games on the weekends and travel and all the rest. She'd known with grim certainty that there would be more disasters. More problems she wasn't there to solve.

Charlie had quit the next day. She hadn't really talked to Melody since. She also hadn't told her parents that she wasn't going to practice anymore. They'd just worry about her, but she wasn't the one they needed to worry about. She was the one who had everything under control.

"Oh. Right. The Weavers," Ms. Suzuki said. She let out a frustrated sound. "Does no one read the memos? I've got to hop on my computer. I promise I'll be done before bedtime." She was already striding up the walk as she said it.

"Why do you say they're weird?" Charlie asked Mr. Crispin.

"I don't know. Just something about them bugs me," he said with a shrug. "I'm sure I'm overthinking it."

"Yeah. Probably," Charlie agreed, but it was getting harder to believe.

"Well, I'll let you go," Mr. Crispin said, waving a hand. "Good chatting with you."

Charlie, who never really knew what to say during casual conversations, nodded her head vigorously. Juliana made a little sound of vague acknowledgment and drifted up the walkway ahead of her dad, scrolling through photos of K-pop stars and dutifully hearting each one. Melody was only a step behind, but as she went, she turned back just enough to give Charlie a little wave. Charlie waved back, then turned to look at the Weavers' house.

Peter was standing in the living room window, looking

through a narrow crack in the curtains. As she watched, he put his hand against the glass, looking her way, and once again she got the impression that he wanted to tell her something. But then a thin-fingered hand draped over his shoulder, drawing him away.

Charlie had hoped to prove that her suspicions were all in her head. But she was only getting more uneasy.

CHAPTER 7

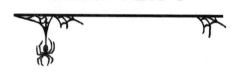

Gideon was feeling better by lunchtime, and this time he stayed that way. Well enough to go to his art class, at least. Charlie watched the Weavers' house, but they didn't come in or out or do anything overtly villainous, so she tried to relax and threw herself into playing endless rounds of *Monster Monster Go!* with Pendleton. He even managed to win a couple of times.

Pendleton finally got up to help Baxter with dinner, and Charlie sat in the living room tweaking her deck. *Not* watching the Weavers' house, even if it happened to be in full view from where she sat. So it was a total coincidence that she saw when the door opened and Peter Weaver emerged. Something about the way he was moving, glancing nervously behind himself at the house before walking quickly down the street, caught her interest. Where was he going?

"Agent Baxter? Agent Pendleton? I'm going to go for a walk," she called.

Baxter's head popped into view. He was wearing a pin-striped apron, and there was flour liberally dusting his broad hands. "Fresh air. Great idea. But be back for dinner in twenty minutes—I'm making biscuits."

"Twenty minutes," Charlie promised. She shoved her shoes on quickly and headed out in the direction Peter had gone. She moved cautiously, eyes darting left and right for some sign of where he had gone.

She came around the corner toward the park at the end of the street and froze. There he was, twenty feet away. He sat on one of the swings, a book in his lap and his head bowed over it. Charlie halted at the entrance to the park, momentarily embarrassed. This was significantly less suspicious than she'd let herself believe. She started to slink backward, but at that moment he looked up.

"Hey," he said, eyes widening a little in surprise. "Charlie, right?"

"Yeah," Charlie said, waving awkwardly. She crossed the grass and stood at the edge of the bark circle around the swings, tucking her hands in her back pockets. Up close, she could see that his hair was mussed at the back and his clothes looked rumpled. Even from here he had a musty smell, like his clothes had been packed away for a long time somewhere dusty. He was still wearing his name tag, but it was curling at the corners. "I was just out for a walk."

Peter nodded. "It's a nice neighborhood," he said.

"Yeah, it's okay," Charlie allowed. They'd moved here right after bringing Matty home, since their old apartment had a no-dogs policy and no exemption for werewolves. She'd lived here longer than anywhere else, but she'd never totally felt like she was part of the neighborhood. "Where did you live before?"

"Pennsylvania," he said. "But we move around a lot."

"Because of your parents' work or something?" she asked.

"Yeah, more or less," he said, and didn't explain further. He rubbed the back of his head. "Hey, sorry I said that thing about you not looking like your siblings. I was just curious, but sometimes I'm not the best at conversation."

"That's okay. Me neither," Charlie said. The trouble with most of her life being classified or unbelievable was that when she *did* get the chance to have a conversation, she couldn't think of anything to say. She walked over to the swings and sat down on the one next to him, swinging back and forth idly. She nodded toward his book. "What are you reading?"

He blushed a little. "Uh, it's called *Watership Down*. It's about these rabbits—and I know that sounds silly, but it's actually—"

"Totally epic," Charlie finished for him, grinning. "It's one of my favorite books."

"Really?" He brightened. "I'm right at the part with Strawberry's warren."

Charlie gave a shudder. Strawberry's warren was one of the creepiest parts of the book, with rabbits that didn't quite act like rabbits and wouldn't talk about the members of the warren who had gone missing.

Everything about the warren felt *off*. Eerie and strange. And then it proved dangerous. Very, very dangerous. The thought made her cold, despite the summer heat.

"I should get home," Peter said. "We're having your next-door neighbors over for dinner."

"Oh," Charlie said, oddly disappointed. He'd probably like Juliana and Melody a lot better than he liked her.

Not that she cared. Not that she had time for friends, she reminded herself.

"It was nice talking to you. Usually it's just me and my parents. I miss . . ." He trailed off and didn't finish. He missed his friends back home, probably.

She didn't get any of the weird vibes off Peter that she did from his parents. Actually, she kind of liked him.

"I'll walk you back," she offered.

They ambled back down the street together, chatting about Hazel and Fiver and Bigwig, and Charlie promised to talk to him about the rest of the book when he was done. Two blocks wasn't far, and she found herself disappointed when they reached her driveway.

The Crispin-Suzukis were walking across the street. Juliana had her nose two inches from her phone as she walked, as usual. Mr. Crispin waved a cheery hello. As they approached the door, it opened, and Mr. Weaver stepped out onto the porch to greet them. Without really thinking about it, Charlie pulled out her phone and went to snap a picture.

Peter stepped abruptly toward her and grabbed her wrist. The camera clicked. Charlie stared at him. He flushed and let go. "My parents don't really like having their picture taken," he said. Then, quickly, "I should go. It was really good seeing you, Charlie."

"You too," Charlie said, blushing a little—he must think she was completely bizarre, randomly taking photos of people like that. Peter loped across the street. Charlie glanced down at the picture she'd taken. It was blurry almost to the point of unrecognizability, but there was Mr. Weaver with his hand outstretched to shake Mr. Crispin's. Was there something strange about his hand? The fingers looked long somehow. Impossibly long.

It must just be because of the blurriness, she told herself, and put the camera away.

Mrs. Weaver was standing in the upstairs window. She was looking down at Charlie, and the angle and the window made her eyes gleam. Flat and white.

Charlie shivered and hurried back inside.

When Charlie went to bed that night, there were three dead spiders on her bedroom floor. Had Miss Sinister been hunting? They were small and green, like the one she'd seen at the Weavers' house. They were all curled up and dried-out looking, but they didn't look like they'd been chewed up. Charlie used a tissue to clean them up and tossed them in the wastebasket with a grimace.

She got into bed, thinking of Peter and his parents. Peter seemed friendly. And he certainly had good taste in books. But she couldn't let go of the sense that something was *wrong*. She pulled up a search on her phone and typed in *Pennsylvania*, not expecting much. The official state website popped up, along with a bunch of random news about politics and weather and things. She was about to shut off the phone when a headline caught her eye.

Disappearance still unexplained: authorities baffled.

She clicked through to the article, heart beating quick in her chest. Three people had gone missing in the small town of White Elm, Pennsylvania, a few weeks ago. The name sounded familiar, but she couldn't remember where she'd heard it. The missing people had all lived on the same street. There was no sign of foul play. It was like they'd vanished into thin air. The article didn't have many details, since no one had any idea what could have happened. No leads, no theories. It was the kind of case her parents would definitely have kept an eye on, but that didn't mean it was connected to the Weavers.

People went missing all the time. Pennsylvania was a pretty big place. Peter and his family might not have lived anywhere near those missing people. But thoughts of that other neighborhood, miles and miles away, kept her awake late into the night.

When she finally slept, she dreamed of the Malice Vault.

It had been before any of her siblings came to live with them. She'd woken up in the middle of the night and heard her mother calling her name. Holding her favorite doll under one arm, she'd padded down the hallway.

"*Chaaaarlie. Chaaarlie,*" her mother had called. She followed the voice into the office, which was bathed in a soft, blue glow. The light was coming from the Malice Vault. The door was open. Charlie had never seen it open. She knew she wasn't supposed to go into it, but her mother's voice was coming from inside.

"*Charlie, come here. I want to show you something,*" her mother said, and laughed. Later, Charlie would realize that while the voice had sounded just like her mother, the laugh hadn't been hers at all. It had been cold and cruel and hungry. But in that moment, sleepy and curious, she had walked right through the open door, and it had slammed shut behind her.

That was where her dreams always began. In the dark.

The dream was impossible. Her parents had rescued her after only a few minutes, but in the dream, time stretched for hours. She dreamed of a rocking chair bound in chains and that knife endlessly dripping blood. She dreamed of closing her hand around the knife, its handle strangely warm against her palm. And then the other little girl was there. *Let's play a game*, she kept saying, and then the dark closed in around her and—

Charlie woke to a sudden pain in her hand. She yelped, snatching it against her chest, and turned on the light. Miss Sinister crouched on her covers, clattering her jaw.

"What was that for?" Charlie demanded. She looked at her hand. It was bright red where the doll had clamped down, and she was pretty sure it was going to bruise. Miss Sinister hissed and skittered backward. Charlie, annoyed, hissed back. Stupid doll. She always acted up when Mom was gone.

Her dream lingered in her mind. Who was that little girl? She almost remembered her.

There was a mirror in the Malice Vault. Agent Pendleton had told her about it once. It made copies of people. And then the copies traded places with the real people. Inside the mirror was a world that changed itself into all sorts of different things, all of them horrible. The mirror thing would take your place for as long as you were inside the mirror, as long as she was *digesting* you.

But the little girl in Charlie's dream hadn't looked *exactly* like her. Not close enough to fool anyone. And she hadn't been in there long enough to get copied. So it was just a dream.

Wasn't it?

There were voices outside. She hopped out of bed and padded over to the window, pulling aside the curtain. Ms. Suzuki and her daughters were emerging from the Weavers' house. Mr. Weaver put his hand on Mrs. Weaver's shoulder, and the two of them waved gaily as the Crispin-Suzukis departed. Charlie reached over to her phone to check the time. It was almost eleven. Their dinner must have run very late. They were all smiles as they crossed the street. Juliana even skipped, her phone nowhere in evidence. But there was no sign of Mr. Crispin. Where was he?

She watched until Ms. Suzuki, Melody, and Juliana were all inside. Mr. Weaver and Mrs. Weaver stayed on the porch. Still waving. They only stopped a good five seconds after the door to the Crispin-Suzuki house had closed.

Then the Weavers went back inside their house. The lights in the windows turned off. Mr. Crispin had never emerged. Everything was quiet, except for the sound of Charlie's breath. And a faint, almost inaudible sound. It was almost like the shifting of autumn leaves in a light breeze. A dry, impatient rustling.

She tilted her head, trying to identify where the noise was coming from. Her eye caught on something on the other side of her bedroom window—a thin green leg, tapping against the glass, seeking purchase. She leaned closer to the window—and then recoiled.

The entire sill outside her window was covered in small green spiders. So many that they were making that faint rustling sound as they scurried back and forth and over each other, their tiny legs tapping and testing.

Like they were looking for a way in.

Charlie leaned her weight on the top of the window to make sure it was secure. There was no way they could get in through there.

Was there?

From the end of the bed, Miss Sinister growled. Her eyes glowed, and she clacked her wooden jaw.

"I don't like this," Charlie told Miss Sinister. The doll growled again, as if she agreed.

CHAPTER 8

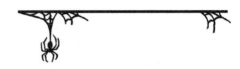

Somehow, Charlie managed to sleep, despite knowing the spiders were there on the other side of the window. She woke with the sun shining through the gap in the curtain and groaned. Her head felt stuffed with fluff, and her eyes were gummy. The sounds of cartoons filtered up from downstairs—*Monster Monster Go!: The Show!*, judging by the theme song.

She'd gotten up, yawning, and put on pants, still yawning, before that struck her as strange. She always woke up before her siblings on Saturdays. Gideon slept like a rock, and Matty wasn't bothered by the sound of the lawn mower, so they always snoozed longer than she did. Opal didn't like to be up by herself, so she always waited for Charlie.

Charlie checked the time. It was 8:30. And the yard next door was quiet. No sign of Mr. Crispin and his top-of-the-line lawn mower, which he'd named Vera, or his hedge trimmers or watering can or wheelbarrow.

Charlie made her way downstairs with a feeling of growing dread. "Hey, did you hear Mr. Crispin mowing the lawn earlier?" she asked Gideon, who was fully absorbed in the show and didn't reply until she repeated herself.

"Ummmm . . ." he said, his eyes twitching back toward the screen. "No?"

"And that doesn't seem weird to you?" Charlie asked.

Gideon rebalanced the heaping bowl of cereal that was in his lap. "Nope."

Charlie sighed. Matty slouched in from the kitchen, a toaster pastry in one hand, his other hand scratching at his ribs. "Did you see Mr. Crispin yet today?" she asked him.

He crammed a third of the pastry into his mouth with one bite. "No."

"He's out there every Saturday," Charlie said.

"So? He decided to sleep in," Matty suggested, then went back to scratching, this time scratching at the base of his skull with a scowl.

"For the first time in three years?" Charlie asked, huffing with annoyance. "I'm going to go see what's going on." The weird green spiders, Gideon getting sick, now Mr. Crispin neglecting lawn care—it was all getting harder and harder to ignore.

"Where are you going now?" Pendleton asked, coming down the stairs. Even on his day off he was wearing a dress shirt.

"I'm, um," Charlie said, and her brain ground to a halt. "Going to go see my friend Melody?" she suggested. Matty gave her a skeptical look. He might not be able to hear what she was saying, but he could tell when she was lying.

"Bring her some cookies, would you? Bax made enough to feed an army, and I'm supposed to be cutting back on refined sugar," Pendleton said, adjusting his cuffs.

"Good idea," Charlie said, relieved that he'd provided her with the excuse she needed for showing up on the Crispin-Suzukis' doorstep.

Matty followed her into the kitchen, polishing off his pastry and flicking the crumbs on his fingers into the sink. "I'm coming with you," he said.

"Why?" Charlie demanded. She grabbed a plate and started loading it with cookies.

"You know how much I like horror movies. Watching you try to talk to people is the next best thing," Matty said, and she gave him a death glare. As he didn't drop dead, she could cross "kill with the power of annoyance" off the list of remaining possible powers she might still develop.

"Let me see your eyes," she commanded. Tomorrow night was the full moon. If Matty was already getting close to shifting, he couldn't leave the house. When he shifted intentionally, which he could do whenever he wanted, he kept all his thoughts and human self. But if he lost control, human Matty vanished, his wolf taking over completely. He wasn't any meaner as a wolf than a boy, but he could get into a truly impressive amount of mischief.

Matty leaned in with his eyes comically wide for her to inspect. Only a few little flecks of amber. "I'm good. Promise," he said.

With Baxter's confections piled high, Charlie and Matty cut across the front lawn. Charlie rang the bell. It was one of those smart doorbells, and after a moment a voice came through the speaker. Juliana.

"Hi?" she said in a distracted tone. Charlie looked through the glass panels beside the door. She could see Juliana in the hall, and if Juliana turned around, she'd see them, but instead she was using the display mounted to the wall to talk, her phone in her other hand.

"Baxter made way too many cookies, so we thought we'd bring you some," Charlie said, lifting the plate into the camera's view.

Juliana's head swiveled around, her eyes fixing on the plate. This was not the first Excessive Baking Incident that the Crispin-Suzukis had benefited from. She'd tasted Baxter's cookies before. "Come on in!" she said with sudden enthusiasm, and even put her phone in her back pocket as she crossed to the door. She stretched out her hands eagerly to take the cookies.

No way Charlie was messing this one up again. "I promised I would bring the plate back," she said.

"Oh. Okay," Juliana said with a shrug, and waved them inside.

The interior of the house was immaculate; Mr. Crispin took his house spouse job seriously. It smelled of lemon cleaner, but Charlie was looking for another scent: cut grass. And she couldn't detect even a hint of it.

"Is your dad home?" she asked Juliana.

"Yeah, I guess," Juliana said. She set the cookies down on the counter and reached up to get one of their plates. With her other hand, she pulled out her phone and let out a dreamy little sigh as she scrolled past a picture of a boy with thick black hair and a million emojis plastered around him.

"Where is he?" Charlie asked. Matty wandered over to look at the pictures on the wall.

"I don't know. Upstairs or something," Juliana said. She started transferring the cookies over.

Footsteps sounded on the stairs, but they were too light to be Mr. Crispin's. Sure enough, it was Melody who traipsed into the room, clad in pajamas that were covered in pink cartoon cats. When she saw Matty and Charlie she froze, eyes wide.

"Uh, hi!" she squeaked. Her eyes darted between the three of them. "I didn't know we had company."

Even though they were identical twins, the girls were easy to tell apart. Juliana kept her hair long and wore little sapphire studs in her ears, and she had started to wear a little bit of makeup. Melody had short, tousled hair, and her knees and elbows were always scraped up from playing lacrosse.

"It's good to see you. How are you?" Melody said slowly, painstakingly signing at the same time. Matty, who had been tuned out enough that Charlie hadn't been bothering to translate for him, blinked at her.

"I'm good," he signed back after a moment. "You sign?"

"I'm learning. I watched a good video on . . ." She mimed something that Charlie realized was supposed to be a laptop opening.

"Cool," Matty said, mildly interested.

"I want to learn more. It's fun," Melody signed, getting it mostly right. Charlie sighed, realizing what was going on. As soon as Matty figured it out, he was going to be insufferable.

"Cool," Matty said again.

"You . . ." Melody said. Then she glanced at Charlie helplessly. "Could you ask if he'd teach me more?"

"Sure," Charlie said resignedly. To Matty, she signed silently, "She wants you to teach her more."

"Why?" he asked, brow creased.

"Seriously? Because she likes you," Charlie signed. His brow creased more. Then his eyes widened.

"Wait. Really?" he signed. He looked unsure of what to think.

"Will he?" Melody asked, looking at Charlie. She gave Matty an expectant look.

"Yes?" Matty said. "Yes. Wait, she really likes me?"

"I'll let you figure that out yourself," Charlie told him, and conveyed his answer. Melody grinned.

"Great! Can I text you?"

"Yes?" Matty said. He idly scratched at his side.

"Give her your number, dingus," Charlie told him. While a stupefied Matty exchange numbers with Melody, Juliana held the plate out to Charlie. She already had a cookie in her mouth, her other hand furiously tapping out a text message.

"'Ere oo oh," she managed around the snickerdoodle.

"Wait. I was really hoping to talk to your dad for a second," Charlie said, taking the plate. "Or your mom?"

"Mom had to go into the office," Melody said.

"What about your dad?"

Melody shrugged. "He's around."

"Where?"

Melody frowned. "Somewhere."

"Is he upstairs?" Charlie pressed.

"No. He's not here," Melody said.

"You just said he *was* here," Charlie pointed out, and Melody's frown deepened. She looked at Juliana.

Juliana extracted the cookie from her mouth. "He's out," she said.

"That's not what you said before."

"Dad went out on an errand," Melody said. It was almost like she'd just remembered—and almost like she'd just found out.

"Yeah. An errand," Juliana said. Her eyes drifted back toward her phone. Charlie resisted the urge to snap her fingers to get her attention. She wanted to make Juliana and Melody tell her exactly where their father was—but she suspected she wasn't going to have much luck.

"Well, enjoy the cookies," Charlie said with forced cheer. Matty waved goodbye to Melody, grinning like a dope, and she had to grab him by the shirtsleeve to get him going in the right direction.

"She wants to hang out," Matty said when they were outside. He was still smiling. "Do you think she thinks I'm cute?"

"You're my brother. I can't tell," she told him.

"Objectively." He spread his hands so she could get the full-picture look.

She squinted at him. "Eh. Maybe."

"From you? That means I'm the cutest ever," Matty said, and she went to smack the back of his head. Of course, with his reflexes, he ducked easily. She couldn't help but return his infectious smile. He spent so much time scowling and slouching, it was good to see him cheerful. But then her smile faltered.

"What?" he asked. He itched at his shoulder, frowning a little.

She wished he wasn't so good at reading facial expressions. "I don't know. I guess I'm a little jealous. I wish someone wanted to hang out with me."

His nose wrinkled. "Like boyfriend-girlfriend hang out?"

"No! Just friends," Charlie said. "I don't really have any."

"That's because any time anyone *does* want to hang out, you ditch them," Matty said with a roll of his eyes.

"I don't *ditch* people, I just have things I have to do," Charlie protested.

"You know you don't have to take care of us all the time," Matty said. "We can take care of ourselves a lot better than you think we can. You think we're totally useless, but we're not."

"I don't think you're totally useless," Charlie protested. And she didn't think that. But they needed to be protected.

A tiny panicked part of her wondered what it would mean if he was right. If they *didn't* need her. If the one special thing about her wasn't useful after all. She pushed the thought away.

"What matters right now is that we need to figure out where Mr. Crispin is," Charlie said firmly.

"Didn't they say he was upstairs?" Matty asked. "I was only kind of paying attention."

"They said he was upstairs, and then that he was out. Like they changed their minds," Charlie said.

Matty rubbed his thumb against the side of his nose. That meant he was thinking about smells. He had a way better sense of smell than any human, but most of the time he didn't pay attention to it the way he did when he was in wolf form—the human brain isn't as interested in smells as a wolf's is.

"You know, I don't think I could smell him," Matty said. "He always smells like—"

"Cut grass," Charlie supplied.

"And window cleaner," Matty agreed. The windows of the Crispin-Suzuki house did have a particular sparkle to them. "But the scents were faded. Like he was there, but not for at least a few hours."

Like, maybe not since eleven o'clock last night.

"This is about your weird thing with the Weavers, isn't it?" Matty asked. She looked across the street. The moving truck was still parked out front, though she hadn't seen the Weavers take anything out of it since yesterday.

"There is something going on," she insisted.

"If you really believe that, you should call Mom and Dad," Matty said. His serious expression broke as he scratched frantically at a spot on his ribs, twisting around to get at it. "What is *with* all these bugbites?" he demanded. His eyes flashed amber. Deep amber.

"Matty, inside!" Charlie yelped, and grabbed him by the shoulder. She hustled him up the walk and through the door right in time.

Matty pitched forward. Even as he fell, the air around him was shifting and shimmering, his form blurring as his limbs rearranged themselves and soft fur grew. By the time he hit the ground, he wasn't an eleven-year-old boy but a gangly puppy with fawn fur, deepening to black on his legs and muzzle, almost like he'd stood in a puddle of ink and couldn't resist sticking his face in.

The puppy immediately thunked his bottom down on the floor and set about furiously scratching with his back leg.

So much for Matty being able to take care of himself.

Charlie sighed, setting her back against the door and sliding to the ground. Matty stopped scratching long enough to attack her shoelace. She ruffled his ears. He ducked away with a bark. Even wolf Matty was too cool for her now, apparently.

"There is something going on over there," she said quietly to herself. "But I'm not going to call Mom and Dad. I'm going to handle this myself."

It was Saturday. Three more days until Mom and Dad got back. She could take care of things that long.

She had to.

CHAPTER 9

A ssistant Director Robert Dixon had never wanted to head up the Division of Extranormal Research and Investigation. He'd *wanted* to retire and had turned in the paperwork no fewer than eight times, in fact. Yet somehow, he was still there. Still Mom and Dad's boss—though Mom liked to remind him that, technically, she was a consultant and outside his chain of command.

He was many things. Tall. Imposing. Possessed of a deep baritone voice that could shake pictures off the walls when he got angry. Twenty years ago, he'd been convinced that the Division was at best a costly and foolish endeavor that would produce no proof of the paranormal, and at worst a prank someone was playing on him. Now he kept salt and holy water in his glove box and slept in a room covered in protective magical symbols.

He'd been at the Division even before Dad. He'd read all their reports. If anyone could help Charlie figure out what was going on, he could.

AD Robert Dixon

10:23 a.m.

Hi Assistant Director Dixon, it's Charlie.
Do you have a minute?

For my favorite Greer? Absolutely.

I'm only your favorite because you don't have a
file on me.

Of course I have a file on you.
I have a file on everyone.
I have a file on my mother.
I have a file on my grandmother.
I have a file on my cat.

Oh.

But you produce less paperwork for me than any
of your family and have never caused me to have
to testify before Congress. Therefore, my favorite.
Keep up the good work.
What do you need, kid?

I was wondering, hypothetically, what could make
a person disappear?

You want to know what could make someone
disappear?
Why?

Long story. Not important.
Any ideas?

Sure. You've got your alien abduction. Bigfoot
abduction. Men in black. Genie wish gone awry.
Interdimensional portal. Cursed Mesopotamian
tablet. Sewer monster. Lake monster. Sea
monster. Swamp monster. Killer clowns. Time
paradox. Cults—you've got death cults, demon
cults, occult cults, new age cults, basically any
kind of cult. Witches. The giant Pacific octopus.
Trapped on a ghost ship. Possessed. Possessed
by a ghost ship—could happen. Knocked
unconscious by genetically engineered mushroom
spores. Genetically modified insect swarm.
Genetically modified alligator. Lots of potential in
the genetically modified space overall, really. Fell
in a vat of invisible paint. Stolen by time thieves.
Shrink ray on the highest setting. Unexpected
wicker man festival. Psychically scrubbed from
memory so you forget them as soon as you aren't
looking at them. Mole men. Lizard men. Giant
carnivorous pitcher plant. Giant carnivorous
catfish. Bears. Got lost in Finland. Went hiking.

Trapped in a TV show. Trapped in a haunted painting. Trapped in a mirror. Trapped in a snow globe. Trees. Not sure how they'd be involved but I always feel like we underestimate them. Moth man. Time loop. Wild hunt. Tax fraud.
I could keep going.
Also if the Operative is anywhere nearby, it was him.
Is the Operative anywhere nearby?

No. I think he's in Paris.

Oh dear.

I checked this morning, Paris is still there!

That's something, at least.
Why are you thinking about disappearances?

No reason.

Don't go causing me any paperwork, Charlie.
We've got a good thing going here.
I'd hate for you to ruin that.

No paperwork, I promise! Just a thought experiment.
So purely hypothetically, do any of those

disappearances have anything to do with spiders?

Did I say genetically modified spiders? Because
they should definitely be on the list.
Huh. You know, actually, that rings a bell.

Really?

Yeah. But I can't think of why. It's on the tip of my
tongue.
Anyway, I've got to go.
My phone's ringing, and the number's French.

Uh-oh. You should probably deal with that.

I swear if that man has caused another
interdimensional incursion . . .

Let me know if you remember what the thing
was? With spiders?

Sure thing. Stay out of trouble.

Always do.

Sitting on her bed, Charlie stared at the list, head spinning. She
was pretty sure Mr. Crispin wasn't in Finland. And there weren't
any sea monsters this far from the coast. Alligators seemed un-

likely. She supposed the Weavers could be in a cult. That might explain how weird they were being. Though the cultists she'd met hadn't been able to go three seconds without talking about their grand, glorious plan to chart the path to the demon world and overthrow the rule of Man, blah blah blah, etc.

The sound of an engine starting up brought Charlie to the window. The moving truck was pulling away from the curb, and the Weavers' beige sedan was following right behind it. They must be returning the truck. If Mr. Weaver was driving one vehicle, that must mean Mrs. Weaver was driving the other. Was Peter with them? She squinted, but she couldn't tell.

She made her way down the stairs. Pendleton was doing the dishes. Baxter was upstairs helping Gideon put together a 3,000-piece *Space Patrol* mothership Lego set. Only Matty and Opal were in the living room. It had taken twenty minutes to coax Matty back into human form, and he'd been sulking ever since. She was glad he'd at least come out of his room.

She waved to get their attention. "I want to go over to the Weavers' house," she signed, keeping an eye out for Pendleton.

"You are going to completely freak them out for no reason with all of this," Matty said.

"What about Mr. Crispin? Where did he go?" Charlie signed.

"What do you mean?"

"He's gone. Remember?" she said.

Matty's brow wrinkled. "Oh. Right."

Had he forgotten so quickly? That didn't make sense. "I'm just going to peek in the window. Can you cover for me?" she asked.

"There's nothing weird over there. I was inside, remember?" Matty said.

"Just do it," she signed snappishly. "Or I'll tell Mom and Dad you lost control because you were *itchy*."

He glowered at her, but nodded.

"Can I come?" Opal asked.

Charlie considered, then nodded. Opal made a good lookout, with her ability to go through walls and turn mostly invisible.

"Where are you going, now?" Pendleton asked aloud, signing with still-wet hands at the same time.

"Charlie's going to take Opal for a walk," Matty signed back casually. Charlie kept her expression blank, but secretly she was impressed at how easily he produced the lie.

"Don't go far. It's getting dark," Pendleton said.

"I can't go far anyway," Opal reminded him.

"And don't forget to have fun," Pendleton said gravely, pointing at her. She ducked her head, turning semitransparent. Charlie avoided Pendleton's eyes, hoping he didn't notice how red her cheeks were. He walked back toward the kitchen, whistling, and Charlie looked over at Matty.

"Thanks," she said.

He shrugged. "Gotta stick together, right?" he said. "You're not going to find anything, for the record."

"We'll see," she replied grimly.

Opal drifted toward the door. Inside the house, she sometimes didn't bother with pretending to need her legs to walk. Charlie was a little slower, since she had to put on her shoes, but soon they were outside in the humid summer air, where Opal turned opaque once again and dropped to the ground.

"We need to get better at lying," Charlie said.

Opal shook her head. "Lying is bad. I don't like being bad."

"Lying isn't *always* bad," Charlie objected. But Opal still looked bothered. "This was just . . . naughty. That's different than bad."

Charlie sometimes forgot how worried Opal was about being evil. She knew that she'd hurt people before—luckily, no one had ever died in the fires she set over the decades, but nobody has a fun time when their house burns down. She hadn't even really been aware of doing it, of course. She always said it was like she was dreaming until Mom found a way to wake her up.

Charlie glanced over her shoulder. Pendleton wasn't in the window anymore. She nodded her head across the street, and the two of them skulked across, looping back the other way. Through the windows of the houses leading up to 1512, Charlie could see her neighbors going about their daily routines. Mr. Khan was vacuuming, Ms. Daniels was sharing a microwaved meal with her cat, and the Adebayo brothers, Luke and Thomas, were playing *Mario Kart* in their front room. But the windows of 1512 were dark, the curtains drawn tight.

"We're just going to look," Charlie said, mostly to herself. She glanced around. No one was watching them. She stole into the side yard between 1512 and 1510. The sun was still up, but the side yard was deeply shadowed. She crept along, Opal trailing behind her. There was one window on this side of the house, but it, too, had the curtains tightly shut.

"Let's try the back," Charlie said.

"What if someone sees us?" Opal whispered.

"We'll come up with a cover story. We can say we're look-ing for Freckles," Charlie said. Opal giggled. A year ago, Matty had gotten out of the basement during the full moon and run off down the street to chase a squirrel. A neighbor had caught him just as Charlie ran up, and when she'd been asked what her "puppy's" name was, she'd blurted out Freckles without think-ing. Worse, Mom and Dad had decided that establishing that they had a dog would be good in case he ever got spotted again, so now Matty went on weekly walks in his wolf form—which was now officially named Freckles.

Matty had never entirely forgiven her.

The backyard was overgrown and choked with weeds. The small patio had cracked pavers, with dandelions springing up through the cracks. All the windows in the back were covered, too. Even the glass panes set in the door.

"Can we go home now?" Opal asked. "You can't see inside."

"*I* can't see inside, but *you* can," Charlie pointed out.

Opal looked stricken. "I'm not allowed to outside the house."

"No one's looking. I'll stand in front of you. Just peek through the door," Charlie urged. Opal looked conflicted.

"It's against the rules," she said.

"I promise if we get in trouble, I will say it was all my idea," Charlie said.

Reluctantly, Opal nodded. Charlie arranged herself as casu-ally as she could to block the view from the neighbors' windows, in case anyone happened to glance out and see a six-year-old sticking her head straight through a door. Opal leaned forward up to her ears, then drew back quickly. "It's super dark. And super messy. Everything's all covered with cobwebs and dust," she said.

Cobwebs and dust? But Matty said it all looked perfectly nice.

Charlie tried the doorknob. Locked. She looked over at Opal, wincing. "Opal. Something is going on here. Matty and Baxter and Gideon couldn't see it, but it's real, and we have to find out what it is. If Mr. Crispin is in there, we have to help him. And that means I need your help. I promise you we will just take a look and then go home, but I need you to unlock the door for me."

"If there's something wrong, shouldn't we call Mom and Dad?" Opal asked.

Charlie shook her head. "No. Because then they'll be worried, and they'll come home, and we don't even know if anything bad is happening. We have to figure this out on our own."

Opal wrapped her arms around herself. "Do I have to?"

Charlie sagged. She needed to get inside. But she couldn't stand seeing Opal so frightened. "No. I'm sorry I asked, Opal. You can go home. I'll find a way in on my own."

"Come home with me," Opal said pleadingly.

Charlie shook her head. "I can't. I have to see what's in there."

Opal looked up at her, worry making tears swim in her eyes. "We're a family now, and that means no one has to be alone," she whispered. Charlie's heart squeezed. That was what Mom told Opal the day they brought her home.

Opal took a deep breath. "I can do it I can do it I can—" she started, and then she ran through the door and the sound cut off.

Charlie waited for one second. Two. She started to get nervous—and then the lock clicked. Charlie opened the door quickly, and Opal grinned at her.

"I did it," she said. The air around her was cloudy with smoke, and Charlie suppressed a cough.

"Great job," she said with only a hint of a wheeze. She stepped inside and closed the door behind her.

Charlie waited for her eyes to adjust to the gloom. She'd been in this kitchen before, years ago. It had been cluttered then; now it was filthy. There was grime packed between the floor tiles, and the wallpaper was speckled with grease. The refrigerator was silent, like it was broken or unplugged. Thick cobwebs hung from the corners.

There were words written on the wall. They were big and black, and scratchy like they'd been done with a bunch of overlapping lines.

THIS IS A NICE, NORMAL KITCHEN, they said. Opal sounded out the words one by one. Charlie swallowed.

She crossed to the fridge and opened it. The interior was dark. A few abandoned bottles of condiments were in the door, but the only other thing was a dusty glass pitcher filled with dirty-looking water. There was a piece of paper taped to it, with the same scratchy handwriting. THIS IS A PITCHER OF FRESH HOMEMADE LEMONADE.

Opal whimpered. "What's going on?" she asked.

"I don't know, but I don't like it," Charlie whispered. She started toward the living room.

"Maybe we should go back," Opal said. "We know there's something wrong now. We should go before someone catches us."

"We know there's something wrong, but we don't know *what*," Charlie said. "We need more information."

The living room was a shambles. The couch was old and saggy. The cushions were split, and it was clear that mice had been stealing the stuffing for their nests—and leaving plenty of poop behind. The floor was covered with dirt and leaves from outside. A big water stain spread across the ceiling and half the wall behind the couch. Also on the wall was the writing that was quickly becoming familiar.

THIS IS A NICE, NORMAL LIVING ROOM, it said.

Charlie tried to swallow, but her mouth was dry. She could hear her pulse thumping in her ears.

She moved through the living room without pausing, passing the entryway. A hallway led deeper into the house. She turned down it, Opal clinging so close that she bumped into—or rather, through—Charlie a couple of times, sending shocks of cold through her.

The first door along the hallway was empty except for stacks and stacks of collapsed cardboard boxes. The tape had been cut, the boxes flattened and piled neatly. On the wall was written THIS IS MR. WEAVER'S OFFICE. There was more writing on the top box in the stack. THIS IS MR. WEAVER'S DESK.

The closet door was open a crack. Charlie ducked inside the room, leaving Opal hovering an inch off the ground out of nerves, and slid the closet door open the rest of the way.

A cascade of small white objects spilled out. Charlie jumped back in alarm with a yelp before she realized what they were—packing peanuts. The entire closet was heaped high with packing peanuts.

She looked behind herself at the cardboard boxes. "They were just full of packing peanuts? There wasn't any stuff?" she said, looking at Opal.

"Why would they move in with a bunch of empty boxes?" Opal asked. Charlie shook her head, just as confused as Opal sounded—confused, and starting to get frightened. There were more cobwebs in here. And not just old, dusty cobwebs. New spiderwebs, too—and along the wall scuttled a bright-green spider, like the one that had almost landed on her.

Like the ones that had been in her bedroom, and outside her window, trying to get in.

"I don't think we should be here," Opal said, but Charlie was already moving, drawn inescapably deeper into the house. She had to see what was here. She had to understand.

The next door was a hall closet. She opened it only a crack and saw that it had been filled three feet deep with more packing peanuts. She eased it shut again before they could come spilling out. There was a bathroom—THIS IS A CLEAN AND FUNCTIONAL BATHROOM. Then there was the master bedroom. More boxes. More packing peanuts. More writing.

THIS IS MR. AND MRS. WEAVER'S ROOM.

THIS IS MR. AND MRS. WEAVER'S COMFORTABLE BED.

There was one more room. The small bedroom in the back of the house. Charlie padded down the hallway, her breathing ragged in her throat. The smell of dust had been overwhelmed by the scent of smoke wafting off Opal. Tiny sparks drifted in the air around her now, too, but still Charlie moved wordlessly toward that final door. It creaked as it opened.

She wasn't sure what she had expected. Some grand and horrible final revelation, maybe. But there was only an empty metal bed frame, patchy with rust, more mouse droppings, and those scratchy words on the wall, taped to the bed frame, and scrawled on top of a stack of boxes.

THIS IS PETER'S BEDROOM.

THIS IS PETER'S BED.

THIS IS PETER'S DESK.

There were a few loose sheets of paper on the box-pile "desk" as well. Charlie wandered over to them, feeling weirdly disconnected as her pulse raced.

THIS IS PETER'S SCHOOLWORK.

"It's like they're telling us what we're supposed to see," Charlie whispered. The words in the front room. Wasn't that exactly what Matty had said? *A nice, normal living room. A pitcher of fresh homemade lemonade.* Those were exactly the words he'd used.

The front door opened. Charlie froze. She hadn't registered the car engine outside, but now her memory filled it in for her. The Weavers were back. Charlie looked frantically over at Opal. Eddies of sparks flew around her, her eyes wide.

"Go," Charlie whispered.

"But—"

"Just go! I'll be okay," Charlie told her firmly, and with one last panicked look at her, Opal darted straight at the wall and through it, leaving behind a smudgy scorch mark. She'd be at the back of the house now. She could sneak around the front, Charlie told herself. But what about Charlie? The only way out of the house was right down that one hallway and out the front door—or all the way through the house to the back. Unless she could get a window open . . .

She scurried to the bedroom window. It was painted shut. She put a hand over her mouth to stifle her moan of dismay. Voices sounded from the hallway. They were odd and raspy, and Charlie couldn't make out the words. And they were moving toward her down the hall.

She looked around frantically. She needed a place to hide, but the only things in the room were the boxes and the bed frame—and the closet.

The closet door was open a few inches, and there weren't any packing peanuts spilling out of it. She hurried over. Opening the door another two inches, just enough to fit through, she squeezed inside and eased the door shut behind her. In the dark, her breath was impossibly loud. She struggled to keep it slow and quiet. She braced her fingertips against the closet door. She could feel splintery grooves in the wood—like something had been carved there.

Cautiously, she pulled her phone from her pocket. She didn't dare use the flashlight, but she thumbed on the phone so that the dim glow of the screen itself illuminated the back of the closet door. There were letters written in a different handwriting than the last—sloppy letters that looked somehow less like a command and more like a plea.

THIS IS PETER'S HIDING PLACE.

A hand clapped over her mouth.

CHAPTER 10

Charlie didn't scream. She wanted to—her whole chest ached with the effort of keeping it in. The hand stayed pressed against her lips as the rustling, rasping voice drew closer, accompanied by a strange *click-click-click-click*. She turned her head slowly. Her phone had gone dim. The only light came from the seam under the door. All she could make out was a dark figure, her height, standing in the darkness.

Peter.

"*Daaahhhrrrliiinnnggg,*" the raspy voice said, the first thing Charlie had been able to understand.

Peter raised a finger to his lips. Charlie managed a frantic nod, and he dropped his hand from her mouth.

"*Peeeteeeehr. Where have you gotten to, mmmmmy dahhhr-ling?*" the voice called. Was that Mrs. Weaver? She could almost hear the syrupy tones of the woman's voice behind those dried-out syllables. "*Hiiiiding agaaaain? Nnnnaughty Peeeteeeeehr. Hhhhave your ffffun. Thhhen come to dinnnnner.*"

The clicking moved out of the room once again. Elsewhere in the house, a door opened and closed. Peter slid his hand into

Charlie's. She started to pull away, but he squeezed her fingers quickly, like saying *please*, and she let him clasp her hand in his. He stepped past her and gently pushed open the door. Light spilled across them both, making Charlie squint. The room was empty, except for a fresh bloom of webs in one corner, tiny green spiders spilling across the threads. Peter pulled her forward. At the door he peeked out, pausing before hustling forward once again.

Charlie let him lead her. Her head whipped back and forth as she searched for signs of his parents. Peter seemed calm, but tense, focused on moving quietly. And he'd been hiding. Whatever his parents were doing, he had to know about it—but maybe he wasn't part of it.

The living room was empty. Nothing moved in the kitchen, either. Peter carefully unlocked the front door and eased it open, then turned to Charlie at last.

For once, he wasn't smiling. His face was pale and his expression drawn.

"Go," he whispered. "Before they realize you're here."

"What's going on here? What are they? Are they really your parents? Where's Mr. Crispin? Are you in danger?" Charlie asked.

Peter only shook his head. "It's not safe. Don't come back. And watch out for the spiders. Here." He took something from his pocket. It was a small piece of polished amber, the size of Charlie's thumbnail, threaded on a braided leather cord. He lifted it over her head, letting it settle around her neck. "They won't bite you if you're wearing this."

She caught his hand. "I can help. Just tell me what's happening."

"You can't help. No one can help. Just save yourself."

A scratching, scuttling sound reached Charlie's ears. It sounded like it was coming from beneath them.

"Go now," he urged, and pushed her out the door. She stumbled back. Peter shut the door on her, and she heard the lock slam home.

Half in a daze, Charlie made her way across the street. The streetlights were coming on. In every house along the block, families were going about their normal nightly routines. It didn't seem possible that she could be the only one who knew what was happening in the house behind her. What was hiding there.

"Opal?" she called softly. "Opal, are you there?"

The air shimmered beside her. She could just see the outline of her sister—the curve of a cheek, the tumble of her hair. The scent of smoke wafted around her.

"I'm here," Opal said, her voice echoing, as spectral as the rest of her. "Are you okay?"

No, Charlie almost said. How could she be? But she swallowed down her fear. "I'm not hurt. Let's get inside."

Opal stayed mostly transparent until they were safely through the door, and then she rushed back into being visible. The effect was like dye being poured into a cup of water. The air around her was still swirling with sparks and smoke, and even though Charlie's heart was pounding and there was a horrible bitter taste in her mouth and she could barely remember how to breathe, she knelt down in front of the little ghost.

"You're safe," she told her, holding out her hands palms up. Opal took in sharp, short gasps, her eyes flared wide. Her outline shook. A bright, fiery line sketched itself across her cheek, and ashes flaked from her skin. She was panicking. "Opal. Look at me. Look at my eyes," Charlie instructed, her own voice shaking.

Opal drew in another sharp breath but did as she was told. Her eyes were turning black at the edges. Charlie kept her eyes on her sister while she calculated the distance to the entryway fire extinguisher. She could get there in four steps.

"Your name is Opal Marie Thompson Greer. You are six years old, and you are at home, safe, with your family," Charlie said. "What's your name?"

"Opal," the girl managed. "I'm home and I'm safe. I'm home and I'm safe."

"And?"

"And I'm not alone," Opal said, her voice shaking. She stretched out her hands and lowered them above Charlie's. For a moment they overlapped, Opal's hands and Charlie's. Charlie's bones went cold. Her skin began to burn. She held still, and a moment later the heat faded, and Opal's hands became solid. Only for a moment. Long enough to feel the touch.

The smoke dissipated. Opal's eyes cleared, and the sparks vanished. Opal shuddered—but she was calm again. Charlie gave her a crooked smile.

"There you go. Good job," she said, relief like a cool balm on her skin. Her palms were red, like she'd gotten a bad sunburn.

She knew they'd be smarting for a few days. She dropped them quickly, before Opal could see. She always felt bad when one of them got hurt, even a little bit.

It was only then that Charlie realized they had an audience. Matty and Gideon were standing in the hall, eyes wide.

"I smelled smoke," Matty said. "What happened?"

Baxter's and Pendleton's voices drifted from the kitchen. Charlie stayed silent as she signed her answer. "I was right. The Weavers aren't what they seem to be. I'll tell you everything upstairs."

Matty leaned back, checking on Baxter and Pendleton. "We shouldn't all go up at once. Stagger it so it's less suspicious. I'll go first."

"Meet up in my room," Charlie signed. Matty's room was technically a little bit bigger but was always a disaster zone of dirty clothes and the vintage video game systems he liked to take apart and repair.

Matty threw her a thumbs-up and slouched toward the stairs, hands in his pockets in perfect "surly preteen" mode.

Gideon followed soon after, and Opal drifted straight upward, skipping the stairs altogether. Charlie waited another couple of minutes before she strolled as casually as she could toward the stairs.

"How was the walk?" Pendleton called from the kitchen. Charlie froze in the hallway, turning toward them with a creaky smile.

This was it, she thought. She could tell Pendleton and Baxter what she'd seen. She could tell them about Mr. Crispin and the spiders and the strange writing and Peter's terror. And then they would call Mom and Dad, and the Division would take care of everything.

Except . . . it was her job to take care of her family, and that meant Mom and Dad, too.

"It was nice. Just went around the block. It's good to get Opal out of the house. You know, since she's anchored here and all. Can't really leave a lot!" Why was she talking so much? It was like she'd started saying words and they just wouldn't stop.

Pendleton looked over the rim of his mug at her. "Uh-huh. I see. Anything interesting happen?"

"Ha, no," Charlie said, the syllables blurting out of her. She wished she was a ghost like Opal so she could sink through the floor. "Anyway, I'm going to go upstairs. Lots of homework, you know."

"It's the summer," Pendleton noted, eyebrow raised.

"Special summer project. Extra credit. G'night!" Charlie said, and fled before he could ask any other questions.

"Good night!" Baxter called after her, his rich baritone cheerfully oblivious to her panic. At the top of the stairs, she paused and tried to get her pulse back under control. Delving into a freaky abandoned house probably owned by monsters? Sure, fine. Lie to an authority figure? Time to panic.

Clearly, she was not ready to do this for a living.

All she wanted to do was collapse onto her bed, but when she walked into her room, it was occupied. Matty was sprawled across half of it, while Opal had tucked herself up on the pillow, arms around her legs. Gideon was at her desk, nervously flipping a ballpoint pen around in the air in front of him, which left Charlie the options of sitting on the floor or pacing nervously.

Charlie went with nervous pacing.

"We are in big trouble," she said. All too aware of the agents downstairs, she didn't speak aloud as she signed. "The Weavers are definitely *not* normal. I'm not sure they're even human."

"Don't be ridiculous. They're a nice, normal family," Matty said, frustrated.

"No, they aren't," Opal said. "The house was all dirty and empty."

Matty shook his head. "Back me up here, Gideon. It was perfectly nice and normal inside."

"Yeah. It was a nice, normal house," Gideon said. The pen swung back and forth, back and forth. Charlie snatched it out of the air.

"You both keep using exactly the same words, do you realize that?"

Matty shrugged. "That's what it was like. Why should I need different words?"

"Tell me *exactly* what you saw," Charlie said, fixing him with a look. "What did the living room look like?"

"It was a nice, normal living room," Matty said.

"Specifically," she pressed.

Matty's hands hovered in the air. "Nice," he signed again, frowning. "Normal."

"What color was the couch?" Charlie asked.

"I don't know," he signed, and his brow creased. Charlie's

heart thudded in her chest. This was *not* normal. Not one bit.

"What about the kitchen?" she asked, turning to Gideon.

"It was . . . a nice, normal kitchen?" Gideon said. His eyes went a bit unfocused. "There's . . . it's . . ." But his hands hovered in the air, fingers shaking. "I can remember it. But I can't describe it. I don't understand."

"What color was the wallpaper?" Charlie asked.

"Yellow," he said. But then he frowned. "Green. No, there wasn't any wallpaper. The walls were white. Blue. They were—"

"Okay, stop. Don't try to describe it anymore," Charlie said, catching his hands in hers. They trembled, and she gave them an encouraging squeeze before letting him go. "What about . . . Matty, how did it smell?"

He closed his eyes and inhaled deeply, as if trying to remember. "It smelled like . . . dust," he said. "And maybe something rotten. But I don't understand. I would have noticed that, and I didn't remember it until just now."

"I could feel something," Gideon said. "Like a buzzing in my head. What's going on, Charlie?"

"The Weavers did something to fool you into seeing what they wanted you to," Charlie said. She told them about what she and Opal had seen, and about the writing on the walls. When she got to the spiders, Gideon reflexively itched at the bite on the back of his hand.

"At least you only have one," Matty said. He lifted up his shirt, and Charlie sucked in a breath. His ribs and stomach and back were absolutely covered with little red bites. He'd already scratched the tops off a bunch of them, and they were scabby and irritated.

"Pendleton has one, too," Charlie said.

"What about Baxter? Did anyone notice him scratching?" Matty asked. Everyone shook their heads. But then, Baxter got hurt kind of a ridiculous amount and never complained about it. He might not even have noticed a bugbite.

"We don't know exactly that the spiders are part of it, but Opal and I are the only ones for sure without bites, and we're the ones who saw what's really there. So I think it's a good theory," Charlie said. "But I haven't even gotten to the weirdest part."

She quickly summarized what had happened after Opal left the house. It was news for Opal, too, and the girl's eyes got wider and wider as Charlie told the story. When she held out the amber necklace for the others to inspect, Gideon touched the stone with the very tips of his fingers and made a little sound of surprise.

"Oh! It's buzzy," he said.

"What kind of buzzy?" Charlie asked.

He screwed up his face, thinking. "When I was little, one of the games we played was 'Things in Boxes.' They gave me a bunch of boxes with things in them, and I was supposed to pick them up one by one and say what I felt. Most of the time I didn't feel anything, but sometimes they were buzzy, and then I would get a treat."

"Sounds like they were using you to identify artifacts," Charlie said. That made sense. The people who had raised Gideon when he was little were rogue agents from A.D.E.P.T. Director Winter had teamed up with Mom and Dad to take them down, and rescued Gideon along the way.

"So Peter's a good guy?" Opal asked.

Charlie hesitated. One thing she'd learned was that "good guy" and "bad guy" didn't always match up with reality. Like the Operative—he was super scary, and he'd worked for people who her parents were trying to stop from doing bad things, but after Dad had saved his life, he'd switched sides, and now he was like an uncle to them. An uncle who randomly sent Christmas presents in July that were usually deadly and once took her out for ice cream and a detailed lesson in how to use a variety of alien weaponry, but still. And most people thought that monsters were bad, but those same people would say ghosts and werewolves were monsters—and Matty and Opal weren't bad at all. Even if Matty was a pain in the butt sometimes.

But then there were the people who seemed nice, before they hurt you. Like when Charlie had really liked the new agent working with Dad, but then it turned out she was part of the whole demon-cult thing. Big disappointment.

"I don't know if Peter is good or bad or in between," Charlie said. "But he was hiding from Mrs. Weaver, and he helped me get out. Plus he gave me this to protect me."

"How do you know it's to protect you? Maybe it's to make sure they can find you and eat you," Matty said, a little unkindly. Charlie covered the necklace with her hand and glared at him.

"He seems different," she said stubbornly. "And if he wanted to let them eat me, he could have just told them I was there.

Besides, he told me he was reading the part about Strawberry's warren, which is all about how things *seem* okay, but there's something really bad happening. I think maybe he was trying to warn me."

"I think he's good," Opal said.

Charlie gave a little nod. She wasn't ready to trust Peter yet—but she wanted to. He'd helped her. She couldn't help but like him for that, at least a little. "We need to find out exactly what Mr. and Mrs. Weaver are. And what kind of threat Peter was talking about," she said.

"We should tell—" Gideon started, but Charlie cut him off with a raised hand.

"We are going to handle this ourselves. Okay? No adults. No Division. No Mom and Dad," she said.

"That's ridiculous. We're just kids. What are we supposed to do?" Matty asked.

"Pendleton and Baxter can't even see that there's anything wrong with the Weavers," Charlie reasoned, knowing even as she said it that it was weak. Not interrupting Mom and Dad's vacation had been one thing when she didn't know what was happening. Now that Peter had suggested their lives were in danger, it was silly to keep the secret. But still she set her jaw stubbornly.

Mom and Dad had trusted her. Her siblings didn't understand. They were either too young, or in Matty's case too distracted by his own angst, to realize just how hard things had been getting. Mom was in bed before Gideon most nights, or never came out at all because of her headaches—headaches that used to only happen after a really bad case. Meanwhile, Dad never slept. When she got up in the middle of the night for a glass of water, he was always in the office, poring through files. There were always more people who needed help. More people in danger.

They gave everything to their work and everything to their kids, and Charlie was worried there wasn't anything left over. They weren't happy anymore. They were always stressed. Dad snapped when he didn't mean to, and Mom cried when she thought no one would notice, and Charlie just wanted everything to be better.

She wanted the vacation to make everything better. So they couldn't tell Pendleton and Baxter. It would ruin everything.

Opal put her hand on Charlie's wrist, cold as winter. "Charlie. We have to tell them. Mr. Crispin is missing. We could be in danger. Mom and Dad have to know."

"It's just a vacation," Matty said.

Charlie's lip trembled. She looked away, embarrassed, as tears pricked her eyes. If she called Mom and Dad, it meant she'd failed them.

It meant she wasn't enough.

Maybe she wasn't special. Maybe she didn't have abilities or powers, and maybe she'd quit the lacrosse team, and yeah, she hadn't told Dad yet because he was going to be disappointed, but he would try to hide it and he would tell her it was okay even though it wasn't, and maybe she wasn't amazing at art or science or math or anything else, just good, just *fine*, maybe she wasn't anything remarkable at all—

This, though, she could do. She could be useful.

But they trusted her, more than anything, to be responsible. And the responsible thing was to get help. Maybe she could convince Baxter and Pendleton not to call Mom and Dad. Maybe they could get AD Dixon and the Division to handle things without ruining the vacation.

"Okay," Charlie said, surrendering. "We'll tell Baxter and Pendleton what's going on."

CHAPTER 11

Baxter and Pendleton were still at the kitchen table. Baxter had his reading glasses on and was thumbing through a well-worn copy of *Jane Eyre* while Pendleton took notes of some kind in his notebook. When Charlie entered, her siblings trailing behind, both agents looked up, and Charlie froze like a deer in the headlights.

"Hey, kids. Need something?" Pendleton asked. He clicked the top of his pen and spun it around his thumb.

"Um," Charlie said eloquently. Baxter carefully placed a bookmark between the pages and set down his book, folding his hands on it and looking over his reading glasses at her.

"Let me guess. You've realized that I forgot to make dessert. And you are absolutely right. I don't know what I was thinking."

"It's not that," Charlie said.

He sat back. "I assumed from your serious expressions it had to be dessert related."

"It's about the Weavers," Charlie said.

Pendleton and Baxter exchanged a look. Charlie paused.

What did that look mean? A prickle traveled down the back of her neck.

"What about the Weavers?" Pendleton asked curiously.

Charlie glanced behind herself, but the others were all still clustered near the kitchen door, letting her take the lead.

"They're using some kind of hypnosis or mind control to make everybody see things that aren't there. The house is actually empty. And Peter said—"

"Miss Charlotte, it's not polite to make up stories about your neighbors," Baxter said, sounding disappointed in her.

"I'm not making it up. Everything you saw inside that house was a lie," she explained, trying to sound calm and professional—trying to sound like Dad would, if he was explaining this. Even though she was so nervous her hands were shaking. "I went in there myself, and I saw the truth."

"The truth is, the Weavers are a nice, normal family," Agent Pendleton said. He clicked the top of his pen. The tip shot out.

"That's just what they're making you think," Charlie insisted. "If we go over there, I can prove it to you." She wasn't totally sure how just yet, but she'd figure it out.

"That won't be necessary. We already know all about the Weavers," Baxter said.

"You do?" Charlie asked, confused.

"Of course we do. They're nice," Baxter said.

The pen clicked. "And normal," Pendleton said, a warning tone in his voice. The pen clicked. Charlie fell back half a step as her eyes flicked between them. This wasn't just them seeing something that wasn't there. This went deeper.

As Charlie watched, a tiny green spider climbed out from Agent Baxter's shirt collar. It scuttled across his throat and vanished back into his shirt on the other side. Pendleton scratched at his wrist. A cluster of tiny bites peeked out from his cuff.

"It's very important that we be good neighbors," Pendleton said. "Your mother and father have entrusted you to our care, so it's our job to make sure you're being . . ."

"Neighborly," Baxter finished. They smiled identical smiles.

"That means no telling stories," Pendleton said.

"And no bothering Mr. and Mrs. Weaver," Baxter added.

"Or there will have to be consequences," Pendleton concluded, and they both stared unblinkingly at Charlie.

"You're right. I'm sorry," she said, struggling to keep her voice steady. "I won't bother them again. Or you. About them. I'm just going to go upstairs. To my room. To read."

"Nothing like a good book before bed," Baxter said approvingly. He opened *Jane Eyre* again, ran his finger down the page, and then made a satisfied *ah* as he found his place. Pendleton went back to writing.

Charlie's siblings stared at her from the doorway. Charlie walked stiffly out of the room, thinking *act natural* to herself and somehow completely unable to manage it.

They thundered up the stairs together. Back in Charlie's room, they all stared at each other.

"Why didn't you try to convince them?" Matty asked.

Charlie had assumed everyone would be on the same page, but Matty was looking at her in complete confusion.

When she'd been down there, everything Baxter and Pendleton had done and said seemed sinister and almost threatening. But now that she was upstairs and a bit calmer, she was suddenly worried she'd overreacted. They hadn't actually said anything threatening, had they? From their perspective, she was the one being unreasonable.

Suddenly she felt very foolish. "I thought they were brainwashed. I thought . . . but I was just overreacting, wasn't I?"

"No, you weren't," Gideon said firmly. She looked at him in surprise. Gideon never said anything firmly. "They were buzzing really loudly. There's something extranormal going on."

"If we got fooled, too, why do we believe Charlie?" Matty asked. "We're not brainwashed."

"Your werewolf stuff lets you heal faster," Charlie reminded him. "Maybe you can resist the spiders' venom, or whatever it is. That could be why they keep biting you so much. Gideon is a tiny bit psychic, so he might be resistant, too. I haven't gotten bitten, and obviously Opal hasn't. We could be the only ones safe from this." She touched the amber necklace self-consciously. If Peter was telling the truth, it should protect her from the spiders—and more and more, she suspected they were the way the Weavers were creating their illusions and tricks.

"Now we *really* have to call Mom and Dad," Gideon said.

What if they called their parents, and Baxter and Pendleton just said everything was fine? "We'll call Mom and Dad, but I want to be able to prove that Baxter and Pendleton are getting mind-wobbled," Charlie said. It was what Gideon used to call it when he was little, and he smiled, ducking his head. "We'll call them, I promise. But let's check the files first. That way we have the info already, in case the mind-wobble makes Baxter and Pendleton try to stop us."

Most of their parents' case files were at the Division, but there were always a fair number at home, too. Their cases were rarely closed, and they both had files they went back to again and again, hoping to spot something they'd missed.

"Makes sense," Matty said, nodding, though by the spark in his eyes he was mostly excited at the prospect of getting to look through the files, which was normally forbidden but always interesting.

"Office?" Charlie said, and the others nodded. "Let's—"

A floorboard creaked in the hall, and she shut her mouth so quickly, her teeth clicked together.

The door opened. Pendleton and Baxter stood in the doorway. They were smiling.

"Look at the four of you. So great to see siblings getting along, spending time together," Baxter said. He sounded like himself. So why did it make Charlie's skin crawl?

"It's getting late," Pendleton said.

"It's not even nine o'clock," Matty objected.

"It's getting late," Pendleton repeated. "You need your rest."

"Sleep is essential for growing children," Baxter said.

Charlie looked between the two men. She didn't want to believe that either one of them would hurt her or her siblings— but she had no idea how extensive the Weavers' control might be. Her mind filled with images of Baxter's hands around her neck—and of how horrified he would be if he ever found out he had hurt any of them.

They needed to do what they were told—for now. Because Baxter and Pendleton weren't bad guys. They needed to be protected, just like her siblings.

"They're right. It's time for bed," Charlie said.

"But—" Opal started. Charlie gave her a look, and she faltered into silence.

"I'll tuck you in," Charlie said. She looked at the agents. "If that's okay?"

Baxter paused, looking almost confused—like whatever was controlling him didn't have an answer for this. "I don't see why not," he said at last.

"Okay, then," Charlie said. She stood, beckoning Matty and Gideon to come as well. Both of them looked puzzled at this turn of events but trooped out. With her back to Pendleton, Charlie signed, "Play along. Stay awake. Wait for me."

She took Opal to the bathroom, where Opal's Minnie Mouse toothbrush and glittery toothpaste waited. She didn't need to brush her teeth, of course, but routine helped keep her grounded, kept her from slipping into that not-quite-dreaming, not-quite-awake space where she'd spent so many years.

All too aware of the agents in the hall, Charlie leaned down to mime the action of brushing Opal's teeth.

"It's going to be okay," she murmured. "Wait until Baxter and Pendleton are in bed, then come to my room."

Opal nodded. Charlie rinsed the toothbrush and then walked with Opal down the hall, the agents' eyes on them the whole way. Opal's room was the smallest one, at the end of the hall. There was nothing about the room to suggest that its occupant was a ghost. There was a bed with pink sheets and a gauzy canopy, a bedside table adorned with a ballerina-shaped lamp, a dresser filled with clothes. There was even a hamper, though no dirty clothes to fill it.

Charlie opened the top drawer for Opal, revealing three sets of neatly folded pajamas. Opal considered for a moment. Then she closed her eyes, faded to semitranslucency, and resolidified wearing purple sushi pajamas that matched the middle set. Charlie shut the drawer as Opal hopped onto the bed—not so much as denting the comforter—and with concentrated effort picked up a teddy bear, crushing it against her chest. Manipulating objects was easier for her than touching people—especially familiar objects like Mr. Snuggles.

Charlie sat next to her, leaning in and keeping her voice low. "We're going to figure this out," she said.

A haze of smoke floated in the air around Opal. "What's going to happen to us?" she whispered. There was a thinness to her voice that alarmed Charlie—a not-there-ness that was more than her usual shyness. More than trying to be quiet. Opal didn't meet Charlie's eyes, and Charlie knew that she was thinking about fading into her dream space. There, she could be safe. Even if it meant losing herself. Losing them.

"Nothing is going to happen to us," Charlie said. She wished that she could gather Opal up in a hug, but instead she reached out, playing with Mr. Snuggles's soft ears. "You're the only one we know for sure can't get bitten, Opal. We need you here.

I promise you, I am going to keep everyone safe, and we are going to find out what's going on. But you've gotta stay."

"I want Mama," Opal whimpered.

"I know. Me, too," Charlie said. She whispered a few last, reassuring words and kissed the air near Opal's forehead. She crept back down the hallway, offering Gideon a small wave as she passed his room.

Miss Sinister was in her room already, curled at the foot of the bed. Charlie changed into pajamas and burrowed under the covers. She opened a book and sat staring at the words, not reading any of them. After a few minutes, Baxter came by to check that she was in bed. Once the door closed behind him, she fished out her phone. There was already a message from Matty.

Mateo Silveira Greer
8:34 p.m.

Do you have a plan?

Same plan. Get in the office. Get the files.

Or call Mom and Dad NOW.

Not yet.

Since when are you NOT worried?
What's up with you and this vacation?

You're being weird about it.

I'm trying to help Mom and Dad, that's all.

He sent another message, but Charlie ignored it and thumbed it off the screen. Tears pricked her eyes. She blinked them away. She hadn't told Matty—hadn't told anyone—about what she'd heard three weeks ago. What she'd seen.

She'd gotten up to use the bathroom. When she walked past Mom and Dad's room, Mom had been sitting at the end of the bed, her head in her hands. Dad sat next to her, rubbing her back.

"I don't know how much longer I can do this," Mom said. "I feel like I'm splitting apart. It's all too much, and it never stops. There's never a single moment when we can just rest, and there's never going to be. And never mind you and I getting any time together—I feel like we're barely married anymore, we're just co-workers who both sleep at the office."

"You're exhausted," Dad had said. "You've been firing on all cylinders for so long I'm surprised you're still standing. You need rest."

"But I can't rest. There's always someone who needs help. Or something wrong with the kids. And before you tell me to let someone else pick up the slack, I can't. You know I can't, because no one else can do what I do."

Dad sighed. "You've got to rest. Otherwise you're going to burn out completely, and that won't help anyone. This trip will be good for you. No work. Just rest, and time for the two of us.

Then we're going to take a look at how to lighten your load."

"Says Mr. Workaholic. You're as burned out as I am—you're just all gruff and stoic about it," Mom retorted. She let out a long breath, dropping her hands. "I can't even look forward to the trip. Because I know something's going to come up, and we're going to have to cancel. Something always comes up."

"Not this time," Dad had said firmly. And then he'd looked up and caught Charlie's eye. He'd given her a sideways nod, a move-along gesture, and she'd scurried away.

Mom and Dad were falling apart. Charlie didn't know what would happen if they did. But she did know that Mom and Dad were all her siblings had. They had rescued Opal from an eternal nightmare of smoke and fire and abandonment. They had given Gideon the first home he'd ever had, and they'd shown Mateo he hadn't become unlovable when he became a monster.

It was Saturday night. They were probably still having a fancy dinner together, with candles and wine and reminding each other every fifteen minutes they'd promised not to talk about work. She'd wait until after looking at the files to call them. Let them finish their dinner, at least.

She told herself that would be enough. But she couldn't help but feel like whatever she did, it would be a huge mistake.

CHAPTER 12

At eleven o'clock, Charlie knocked twice on the wall between her room and Gideon's. There was a pause. If Gideon was awake, he should be passing along the knock. Sure enough, a few seconds later Opal came zipping through the wall, still in her purple pajamas.

"Go see what Pendleton and Baxter are doing," Charlie signed. "Don't let them see you."

Opal nodded in acknowledgment and faded to almost nothing before drifting out into the hall, a thin coil of smoke lingering behind her. Charlie crinkled her nose. Opal's smoke wasn't real smoke, exactly. It didn't linger or leave particles behind, and it wouldn't cause them any problems from breathing it in. But it sure smelled like real smoke until it faded. And when she got scared enough to light things on fire, the fire definitely *was* real. It was going to be tricky keeping Opal calm enough not to singe things.

A minute later, Opal returned, fully visible. "They're asleep in the guest room," she reported. The guest room was downstairs; that meant the upstairs was clear.

"Get Gideon. We're going to the office," Charlie said. She gave Miss Sinister a pat before marching across the hallway to collect Matty, who was still fully dressed and reading a comic book—a horror comic about a bloodthirsty werewolf. "You know Mom doesn't like you reading that stuff," Charlie told him.

He tossed it onto the bedspread with a shrug. "It's not about *real* werewolves. And it's fun."

The book had fallen open to a full-page panel of the werewolf covered in blood and guts. Charlie made a face. "You have a weird definition of fun."

He shrugged again. As he walked into the hall, the light hit his eyes, making them glint yellow. Tomorrow was Sunday. Meaning when the sun went down tomorrow, Freckles would be coming to visit. She cursed the bad timing. His lycanthropy wouldn't be contagious until he was an adult, and he wasn't aggressive to people, but if they didn't want him running into traffic or eating bunnies on the neighbors' lawns, they had to keep him locked up.

That would mean he couldn't help. And he'd be vulnerable if the Weavers were up to something sinister.

There was nothing she could do about it now. Gideon and Opal were already in the office. Opal was sitting in Dad's chair, while Gideon used his abilities to spin it for her as she stifled giggles.

"Shh," Charlie chided, and Opal clapped her hands over her mouth. Gideon held out a hand, and the chair halted halfway through its spin.

"Sorry," he said guiltily. Charlie huffed and rolled her eyes, but she was glad to hear Opal laughing. If it made her less freaked out, maybe a little noise was okay.

"The file cabinets are locked," Matty pointed out. "Unless you know where the key is . . ."

Charlie shook her head. "Any chance you've decided to take up lock picking?" she asked him. He gave her a flat look. "Worth checking." She glanced over at Gideon. "Do you think you could do it?"

He frowned at her. "How would I open a lock?"

"Locks are mechanical. You line up the bumps of the key to the right depth, and it lets it turn," Charlie said. "You can move things with your mind. If you could line them up just right . . ."

Gideon looked doubtful. Matty huffed impatiently. Charlie caught another glimmer of yellow in his eyes. He needed to watch his temper, but pointing that out would only make him grumpier.

"See if you can find a video to show him," she told Matty. Matty pulled out his phone and sat down next to Gideon. Opal tucked her hands under her thighs, her legs swinging freely as she watched them.

The hair on the back of Charlie's neck prickled. She gritted her teeth, refusing to turn. Refusing to look at the big metal door on the back wall. The Malice Vault didn't scare her. That's what she told herself, at least. It had tried to get her, and it had failed, and she would never be that foolish again.

She knew that what happened that night couldn't happen again. The vault hadn't been properly secured before, and now it was. Now there was a much more official process in place for assessing each item and making sure it was thoroughly contained. And many of the items that had been in the vault back then were gone. Some of them, they'd found ways to destroy. Others were in a facility the Division owned, which had all the protections of the Malice Vault—all except for one. Mom. Her Soothe was what kept the things in the Malice Vault truly tame.

Even if they got into the filing cabinet, Charlie reflected, they needed to know what they were looking for. AD Dixon said he thought the spider thing sounded familiar, and he basically never slept. She pulled up her conversation with him.

AD Robert Dixon

11:13 p.m.

I have more questions about spiders.

I thought you were asking about disappearances.

And spiders.
Not disappearing spiders.
Spiders causing
disappearances.

Charlie, is something going
on I need to be worried about?

No, I promise! I'm writing a short story.
Looking for inspiration.

Really.
Okay.

You said that it reminded you of a case.
Do you remember anything more?

I've been wracking my brain since
you sent your message.
It was right before your folks got married.
2009, I think.
Somewhere on the West Coast. Seattle, maybe.
No, Portland. Out in the suburbs.
Some people vanished, and no one seemed to
notice. When the team showed up there was no
sign of what had happened except a bunch
of spiders and graffiti, and an artifact.
I can't recall exactly what it was, but I know we
chucked it in the Malice Vault.
Never found out what was going on.

What about the missing people?

Never found them, either.
The details escape me, but it always
bugged your dad (pardon the pun).

Thanks! That's some great inspiration for my story.

No problem, kid. Just remember one thing.

Don't do anything that would make
you do paperwork?

That's the one.

Charlie said goodbye and closed the conversation. She was not at all sure she was going to be able to avoid causing paperwork, but since AD Dixon couldn't actually fire her or anything, she wasn't too worried about him.

Dixon had said that the case bothered Dad. That at least made it more likely that he'd have the file on hand—he'd want to have it nearby when he got in one of those moods where he puzzled over old cases, trying to see what he'd missed the first time around.

And the file wasn't the only thing that might be here. Her eyes drifted back to the Malice Vault. Was it her imagination, or could she hear the faintest whisper coming from the door?

She shuddered. She was imagining things. There was no way anything could get out of the Malice Vault. Not even the faintest whisper of sound.

Except for that time that it had.

"I'm trying!" Gideon said in a plaintive voice, and Charlie's attention snapped back to her siblings. Matty was shoving the phone in Gideon's face, jabbing his finger at the screen.

"Like this. *Gently,* not shoving it around!" he signed.

"It's hard when I can't see it," Gideon protested. The air

around him was shimmering. Matty let out a low, very inhuman growl, his eyes pure amber.

"Hey!" Charlie dove forward to wag a hand where Matty could see it. "Calm down, both of you. Matty, you're losing control."

"I am not," he protested, baring teeth that were starting to get sharp. Then he clamped his lips shut and crossed his arms angrily, his version of "I'm not talking to you."

Charlie sighed. She should have known she couldn't just let them do it on their own. She sat cross legged next to Gideon, who was hunched over, looking miserable. She put an arm around his shoulders.

"It's okay. You don't have to if it's too hard," she said. Maybe they could find another way to open the filing cabinet.

"I was showing him what to do," Matty said.

"You were bullying him. He can't do it if he's flustered," Charlie said.

"Stop treating us like babies!" Matty replied, and threw his hands in the air. Opal shrank back, smoke spilling out around her.

"You're stressing Opal out," Charlie chided him.

"Fine. You show him, then." He stalked over to the other side of the room and leaned against the wall, glowering. Charlie glowered right back, but turned her attention to Gideon.

"I don't know if I can do it," Gideon whispered.

Charlie squeezed his shoulder. "Remember when you found that butterfly that couldn't fly because its wings were wet, and you used your powers to unfurl them until they dried? You were so, so gentle, and so precise. If you can be so delicate you can save a butterfly, you can do this. Even if you can't see it."

Gideon's brow furrowed in focus. "Okay," he said. "I'll try." She gave him an encouraging smile, shooting a glare at Matty over the top of his head.

Gideon stared. He stared so hard that sweat broke out on his forehead, and Charlie could feel the air pressure changing around them. And then, suddenly, there was a click.

Gideon let out a hiss of triumph, and the drawer slid open.

"One down," he declared. He rolled his shoulders. Charlie gave him a high five.

"You work on the other ones," Charlie said. She looked over at Matty. "Want to help me with the files, or sulk?"

"Obviously I'll help," Matty said, stomping over.

Charlie and Matty pulled out a few handfuls each, doing their best to keep them somewhat organized. Opal came over, but she couldn't read very well—or turn pages easily—so she just hovered (literally) over Charlie's shoulder.

"We're looking for Portland, 2009. Missing people and spiders. I—ah!" Charlie slammed the file she'd been looking at shut.

"What was that?" Opal said, her mouth scrunched up. "It looked gooey."

"Okay, Opal, you're going to keep watch," Charlie said, feeling queasy.

"Why?"

"Because that was a man with his insides on his outsides, and I'm going to be scarred for life, so you *definitely* shouldn't look," Charlie said. She was suddenly remembering that there were a lot of cases her parents wouldn't tell them about, and not just because they were classified.

Matty picked up the file and peeked inside. "Gory," he signed, but didn't look away.

"Ew. Okay, you can have the gross ones," Charlie told him.

"Doesn't have anything to do with us. Just a beast-type cryptid," Matty said. "Ate some Twilight fans in Forks, Washington, and then a hunter got it."

"Ick, ick, ick," Charlie said, shaking her head. He set it aside. The next one was less gross, at least—another cryptid, but this one of the confused-and-lost rather than movie-fan-hunting variety. It had been relocated to a more remote area and equipped with a tracking collar. The next two involved death, but no grisly pictures, and then there was a girl who kept drawing pictures of future events, but only future events that involved cheese. The one after those was an open case involving the spectral figure of a hockey mascot glimpsed at the scenes of disasters as far back as 1875. Charlie stared at the photo of the Hindenburg, the mascot at the edge of the frame, its wild eyes boring into the camera lens, and then slowly set the file aside.

So far, no spiders. And Charlie was wasting time getting interested in all the cases and reading way more than she needed to. Gideon already had the next drawer open and had stopped to help them sort through the files.

"Just look at the dates," Charlie suggested. "2009."

"I can't tell how these are organized," Matty complained. "It seems totally random."

"That's because this is *Mom's* filing cabinet," Gideon said. They all groaned. Mom was many wonderful things, but organized was not on the list.

"I think Dad's the one who would have the file," Charlie said, realizing her mistake.

Gideon looked over his shoulder at the other filing cabinet and sighed. "Okay. Starting over," he said, and scooted across the floor to the other set of drawers.

"Great. And Opal—" Charlie started.

"Make sure Baxter and Pendleton are still asleep?" Opal guessed. Charlie nodded, and Opal flitted off to check.

Gideon got the lock faster this time. They made their way through one drawer, then another. Gideon had popped open a third drawer and was working on the fourth when Charlie opened a file and made a sound of excitement.

November 2009. Portland, Oregon. "I think this is it!" she declared. The front page was a simple one-page summary, written in Kyle Greer's straightforward style. It referred to Leigh Coleman, and it took Charlie a moment to remember it was from before they got married. It was weird to think there was a time before they were married—before they were even *together.* They'd spent seven years secretly in love with each other before they even kissed, even though *everyone* but them knew they should be together. It was basically the best story ever, although Pendleton and Baxter agreed it had been super annoying to live through.

Charlie adored her parents. She loved their story, and she loved that they loved each other so much. She loved how strong and quiet and steady her father was, and how energetic and joyful and sincere her mother was. She loved how both of them, in their own way, would do absolutely anything to take care of the people who needed it, and always tried to do the right thing, even when it wasn't easy.

Even when it was almost impossible.

Charlie opened the file and began to read.

CHAPTER 13

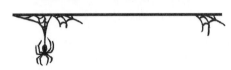

The Clarksons were the first. One day they were there, and the next they were gone, and no one seemed to notice. Not their neighbors. Not their children, who were old enough to mostly look after themselves in any case. It was only later that Special Agent Kyle Greer was able to piece together the timeline and realize that Marion and Donald Clarkson had gone to bed in their two-story house on Primrose Avenue on Friday night. They had set their coffee maker to brew them a pot in the morning, but they'd never touched it. By the next morning, they were gone.

Maria Ramos was the next to vanish, though the exact date couldn't be determined. Her husband continued in her absence without a trace of alarm. Five other people vanished within a five-block radius before out-of-state family and employers began to send up an alarm.

Everyone remembered that the missing people *existed*. It was just that they didn't notice that they were gone. If they were asked, they gave blank looks. When Agent Greer pressed, they acknowledged that the missing people should have been there, and that they weren't—but they weren't the least bit concerned about it and seemed unable to stay focused on the thought for any amount of time, quickly changing the subject.

The final couple to go missing was of particular interest. They had moved into the neighborhood a few weeks before. Their names were Mr. and Mrs. Weber, and no one had anything bad to say about them.

In fact, everyone had pretty much the same thing to say about them.

Edith Darlington, 56 Primrose Avenue: "They seemed like a nice, normal couple."

Frank Wrigley, 60 Primrose Avenue: "They were just a nice, normal couple."

Nicholas Mason, 87 Primrose Avenue: "They were perfectly nice. Normal folks, you know?"

"This is it," Charlie said, reading through the file. It was thin—they'd never found very much, and the case was never closed. The witness statements were repetitive and vague.

"It says they found an artifact?" Matty asked, reading from an awkward angle with his neck craned.

"It was in a shed, in a big spiderweb . . . egg . . . thing," Charlie said. There was just one sheet in the back of the file about the artifact.

Artifact recovered: Large piece of amber, approximately 3" in diameter, containing a large preserved spider. Emits psychic disruption field. When exposed to the field, Agent Pendleton became unresponsive and fell into a stupor.

Recovery was swift once removed from proximity. Threat level high. Use extreme caution.

Remanded to the Malice Vault 1/5/2010.

For further information see file DERI-818.

Charlie uttered a curse word and immediately cast a guilty look at Gideon. The artifact files were all at the Division, which meant they couldn't get to them.

"The thing they found is in there?" Gideon asked, looking at the Malice Vault door with a frightened expression.

"Could that be what they're after?" Charlie mused aloud. "They waited until Mom and Dad were leaving so they could brainwash us all and get into the Malice Vault." It didn't explain what they were or why they needed the artifact, but knowing what the Weavers wanted was at least a step in the right direction.

"Why wouldn't they just make Baxter and Pendleton open it?" Gideon asked. "If they're already brainwashed . . ."

"They can't get in on their own, stupid," Matty signed.

"Hey," Charlie said, cutting a sharp look at Matty. "Be nice. But he's right, Gideon. Only Mom and Dad have the code. Pendleton and Baxter don't have access."

"You're sure no one else knows the code?" Gideon asked.

"Yeah. Only Mom and Dad," Charlie said, her words stiff with the lie in them. Only Mom and Dad were *supposed* to know the code.

But Charlie knew it, too.

She stared at the file open in her lap. Disappearances, suburban neighborhood, no signs of foul play . . . It was just like the article she'd read about the people missing in Pennsylvania. She pulled the article up again. Her eyes snapped to the name of the town. White Elm. It had sounded familiar, and now she remembered why.

The White Elm, case her mother had said. Charlie's gaze flicked to Mom's desk, where the file still sat. *The Almost People.* Could it be connected?

The door creaked. They all jumped, but it was only Miss Sinister skittering in. She clawed her way up on top of Mom's desk and made a muffled growling sound.

"Miss Sinister, what—" Charlie stopped, seeing what was sticking out of Miss Sinister's mouth. She'd caught one of the green spiders. Two of its legs stuck out of her mouth, still waving feebly. "Good girl," Charlie said fiercely.

Miss Sinister preened. Then Opal bolted through the door, panting.

"They're awake! They're coming up! They're already on the stairs," she signed frantically.

"Get back to your room," Charlie told her. She looked at Gideon and Matty. If they ran out into the hall now, they'd get caught. If they waited in here, surely Pendleton and Baxter would check on them in their rooms and realize they were gone.

"Hide," she said. "Gideon, closet. Matty—"

She pointed to the corner near the Malice Vault door, where a large potted plant sat, with a gap between the pot and the wall. It was much too small for a gangly teenager, but a gangly *puppy* . . .

Matty didn't need her to tell him what she meant. He shifted immediately, practically in the blink of an eye. Charlie held her breath, worried that this close to the full moon they'd get Freckles instead of Matty, but he gave a sharp dip of his chin and scrambled to his hiding place.

Gideon ducked into the closet. But none of that would help if the agents checked on their rooms, which surely they would. Unless Charlie distracted them.

Heart hammering, she slid the Portland file back into the filing cabinet. Then she whacked the side of it, hard, making a clang that could surely be heard all the way down the hall. She grabbed a handful of files and started stuffing them back in the drawer as heavy footfalls drew close.

The door opened wide, Baxter's huge hand planted on it. He and Pendleton loomed in the doorway, looking down at her as she leaped guiltily to her feet.

"What are you doing out of bed, Miss Charlotte?" he asked.

She swallowed down her fear. "I . . . I was looking at Mom and Dad's files," she stammered.

"You're not supposed to read those," Pendleton reminded her. He stepped forward. Charlie couldn't help but dart her eyes toward the closet, the bifold door standing a few inches open. Was that Gideon's arm visible in the gap? Pendleton started to follow her gaze. She dropped the files she had been holding, exclaiming at her own clumsiness, and he bent to help her pick them up instead. She tried hard not to glance toward her brothers again—or the file still sitting out on Mom's desk, half-hidden under Miss Sinister's petticoats.

"I'm sorry. I know I'm not supposed to, but they're so

interesting, and I want to work for the Division someday, and the more I know, the better my chances, right? It's not like I have powers, so I have to be the *best* at everything else," she babbled. It had the benefit of being true. She'd never broken into the filing cabinets, but she had sneaked looks at the files Mom and Dad left lying around, and she interrogated them for whatever details they would give her.

"Your parents would be very unhappy to know you were going through their things," Pendleton said. He sounded like himself. Charlie searched his eyes for any sign of outside influence, but he was just frowning at her with a somewhat fond expression. He must believe her.

"I'll put them away. I'm sorry. Please don't tell Dad," she said. Mom was one thing. Mom was a rule breaker by nature. Dad, though—if Dad had an extranormal ability, it was to make *not mad, just disappointed* a deadly weapon.

"It'll be our secret. As long as it doesn't happen again," Pendleton said. "Right, hon?"

"We'll keep it need-to-know," Baxter agreed gravely.

Charlie smiled gratefully. She and Pendleton put the files away and shut the drawer. He hadn't asked how she'd gotten it open, at least. A few steps to the hall and they'd be clear—then she only had to make sure they didn't look into the boys' rooms.

"Let's get you back to bed," Pendleton said. He walked her toward the door.

"Hold on," Charlie said. "I'd better grab Miss Sinister. If she gets locked in here, she shreds things."

Pendleton waved her back, and she hurried to the desk. The

doll hissed at her. She sighed and clamped a firm hand behind Miss Sinister's head. The doll thrashed. Charlie used her flailing to cover up the movement of slipping the file between her chest and Miss Sinister's voluminous skirts.

"Hush," she chided the doll, and Miss Sinister, for once, went still. With her mouth dry, she walked past Pendleton as if nothing was wrong.

Pendleton walked her toward her room. Baxter, behind them, peeked inside Opal's room. Charlie's breath caught, but he stared in for only a moment before easing the door shut again. Opal must be in there. He stepped toward Matty's room.

"Agent Baxter?" Charlie said, halting in the hall. He paused, hand on the doorknob. "Do you think you could get me a glass of water from downstairs? My throat feels really dry." She was so nervous her voice *did* sound scratchy.

"No problem, Miss Charlotte," he said. His hand dropped from the doorknob, and he turned sideways to squeeze past them in the hall.

One down. But Pendleton was standing in the hall outside Charlie's room with his hands in his pockets, clearly with no intention of stepping out of the hall and letting the boys sneak back to their rooms. Charlie stepped toward the stairs like she was just waiting for Baxter to return, then turned to Pendleton, hoping and praying that her brothers would know when to move.

"Agent Pendleton? Can I ask you a question?" she said, wracking her brain for something to say even as the words left her mouth.

"You can ask. Can't promise I'll answer it," he said. He looked tired; there were dark circles under his eyes.

"Right. Um. When you started at the Division, was it hard, not having any powers?" she asked.

"Neither do Baxter or your dad," Pendleton reminded her.

"Still. It must have been scary, dealing with all that paranormal stuff without knowing much about it," Charlie said.

"When I started, I was pretty sure that almost all of it was some kind of scam," Pendleton admitted. "Which lasts up until a psychic criminal is stalking you through your dreams, let me tell you. I was out of my depth. But powers only get you so far, Charlie. Smarts and dedication will get you a lot further, in my experience."

As he spoke, the door to the office eased open. First Matty padded across the hall, his soft paws whisper quiet on the carpet. He nosed open his door and darted inside. Gideon floated out behind him, concentrating furiously as he hovered just above the ground so he wouldn't make a sound.

He vanished into his room just as Pendleton finished talking. The stairs creaked under Baxter's weight, and Charlie tried not to let her relief show on her face.

"That's pretty much what Dad says," Charlie told Pendleton.

He chuckled. "But he's your dad, so you're not going to believe it from him," he said.

"He *has* to tell me that I'm just as special without powers," Charlie said. She'd meant to just distract him, but she *could* use some genuine Pendleton advice right now. Even if he was a bit mind-wobbled.

"The Division has never been Leigh doing the work and Agent Greer tagging along. They've been equal partners from the start. Neither of them could do it without the other," Pendleton said. Baxter reached the top of the stairs, and Charlie took the cup of water from him, keeping Miss Sinister, still oddly compliant, under the other arm.

"Thanks," she said. "Both of you. And I'm sorry about sneaking around."

Something passed over both their faces in the same instant. Pendleton's face hardened. He narrowed his eyes at her.

"Don't do it again," he said, and there was no warmth in his words or his face.

"Do what you're told," Baxter added, and his deep voice sounded suddenly threatening.

Charlie shrank back. They were still under the Weavers' control.

"Good night, Miss Charlotte," Baxter said. Pendleton reached out and closed the door, leaving Charlie in the dim light of her bedside lamp. Miss Sinister began to wriggle in her arms once again, and she released her. The doll thumped to the ground and scuttled under the bed, making grumpy sounds.

Charlie looked down at the file she'd taken from the office. THE ALMOST PEOPLE. The words sent a shiver down her spine.

She went over to her desk and opened the file. It was clearly one of Mom's, not an official Division one: instead of forms and typed-up reports, it was a chaotic scramble of printouts and newspaper clippings and Post-its with scrawled notes and photos. Charlie took out each item one by one and laid them out on the desk. When she ran out of room, she moved to the floor. She stood back and looked at all the photos and scraps of paper and printouts in front of her.

CHAPTER 14

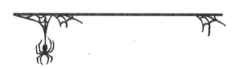

It started with a single photograph. At first it seemed like nothing was out of place. It showed a picnic, men and women and children standing around and laughing with checkered tablecloths laid out over the picnic tables. The faded colors and clothes suggested it was from decades ago. There was a man near the edge of the frame who caught Charlie's attention. Like everyone else, he was smiling. He looked, Charlie thought, like a nice, normal man.

Except for his eyes. Charlie squinted at the photo for a full thirty seconds before she realized what was wrong with them. His eyes were upside down. The photo quality was poor enough that you almost couldn't tell that the lower lids and upper lids had been switched around, except that it gave his face an uncanny quality. If the printed photograph itself hadn't obviously been old, Charlie would have said it was Photoshop. But there were ways to change photos as far back as photos existed, she reminded herself—maybe it was a joke. An art piece.

The man in that photo didn't show up in any of the others. But in each photograph, if she looked hard enough, she found someone with something just a little bit wrong with them. Their mouths were too wide, or only a single lipless line across their faces. One woman's eyes were too large—*just* big enough that it was unsettling. One man was smiling, but instead of teeth he had a single solid curve of enamel.

No one in the photos seemed to notice. They also didn't seem to notice that the strangers—the *Almost* People—were always, always smiling. Even when the photos weren't of picnics and parties, but of fires and accidents and other grim things.

Like Mr. and Mrs. Weaver, beaming in a photo taken of a burning house.

Charlie gasped, then clapped a hand over her mouth to stifle the sound. There was no mistaking them. The photo had a date on it—1999—but Mr. and Mrs. Weaver looked exactly the same age as they were now. They looked the same in almost every way, in fact, except that Mr. Weaver's hands were long and stretched, his fingers bone thin. Mrs. Weaver had two pupils in each eye, and two more eyes dotted along each cheekbone. Charlie's hand shook as she held the photo. The Weavers definitely didn't look like that. She'd seen them up close. But the Weavers of the photo stared back at her, monstrous and alien.

Mom's hand-scrawled notes were stuffed in among the photos, sometimes on Post-it notes stuck to the pictures themselves, other times just tucked in at random.

Mistakes only show up in photos/video, said one. That explained why the other people in the photos didn't notice. Why Charlie hadn't noticed, either.

Twelve of them? read another note. Charlie looked back at

the photos, starting to separate them out into piles. Some of the Almost People were alone, but most came in pairs. They all seemed to be about the same age—thirties, probably, though they had those faces that could easily be ten years older or younger.

The Weavers were Almost People, and they were connected to the case in Portland. There was nothing in the Almost People file about that case—Mom and Dad must not know there was a connection. Charlie's heart beat fast. This was exactly the sort of thing that could crack a case wide open. And she'd found it. Charlie Greer, nothing special, had found a link that Mom and Dad hadn't in over a decade of searching.

Also in the file were three sheets of paper stapled together. It was a list of names, locations, and dates. Some were scribbled out. Some were circled. Many had notes written next to them.

They were people who had gone missing. *Clusters* of missing people, Charlie realized, looking at the addresses and dates—anywhere from one to a dozen people in a neighborhood within a span of a few weeks at most, sometimes only a few days. Like Portland. Like White Elm. Like *here*. The thought sent a bolt of fear through her. What if Mr. Crispin was only the start?

Charlie started typing the names into her phone. Articles popped up for some of them—not many.

No one who had disappeared had ever been found.

What did that mean for Mr. Crispin?

There was an envelope tucked in the back of the file. Charlie opened it and pulled out a stack of photographs and a page of notes in her mother's handwriting. It was a list of names.

Daniela Cooper. Nolan Walker. Rachel Compton. There were dates and locations beside them. The locations matched the clusters of missing people—but these victims must have been different somehow, otherwise why keep a separate list? Charlie flipped through the photographs, all of them labeled with the same names from the list. She froze when she looked at Rachel Compton. She knew her. She'd worked with Charlie's parents. She was a psychic, like Leigh Greer—though not nearly as powerful.

There was a note scrawled on the bottom of the page of names.

Preying on extranormals, it said.

Was that how the Weavers chose their targets? They hunted down people with extranormal abilities—like Mom. Like Matty and Gideon and Opal.

This was serious. This was way more serious than Charlie could even begin to handle on her own. Mr. Crispin had already gone missing, and now it seemed like something terrible must have happened to him. Pendleton and Baxter were hypnotized, or mind controlled, or whatever was going on, and her siblings were in danger, and she should have called her parents a long time ago.

Charlie sat down on the edge of the bed, her head in her hands. She should have called hours ago.

Why had she thought she could handle this all by herself?

Why had she thought even for a second that she was good enough, special enough, to succeed? She wasn't an agent. She didn't have powers. She was nothing. And now Mom and Dad were going to have to come home—*and* they were going to be angry at her for hiding things.

She took her phone out of her pocket. She pulled up Dad's number. Then Mom's. Then Dad's. Which of them would be less mad at her? Did it matter? They'd both find out.

Dad, she decided. He'd be mad. Maybe madder than Mom. But he'd also understand. She'd always been more like her dad—more methodical, more steady. Boring, Matty would say, but then, Matty could probably use a little more boring himself.

The phone rang. She waited, holding her breath, but it went through to voicemail. She couldn't decide if she was relieved or disappointed that she wouldn't have to talk to him. "Dad, it's Charlie. Listen, something is really, really wrong with the new neighbors. There are people going missing—I mean, Mr. Crispin, so at least one person—and you can't trust Baxter and Pendleton because the Weavers—that's the new neighbors— they're doing something to people's minds, everyone's all mind-wobbled, and—" Charlie stopped. She was babbling. She took a deep breath. What would Dad do? "Baxter and Pendleton have been compromised. We need help right away. The new neighbors are the Almost People. I think. Please come home." She stopped. Then added weakly, "I'm sorry."

And then she hung up and called Mom. She got voicemail again and left the same message, though with less rambling this time. They were probably asleep. She could keep calling, but they'd probably turned off their phones. Was there anyone else she could call?

AD Dixon wouldn't be thrilled, but he *would* be able to help. She pulled up his number.

Just as she was about to press the button, her screen lit up with an incoming call. It just said *Unknown Number*. Normally, she would have ignored it, assuming it was spam, but the timing was disconcerting. After the third ring, she answered.

"Hello?" she said, wishing her voice sounded less small.

"Is this Charlie?" the voice on the other end asked. She didn't recognize it, and the words sounded tinny and far away, distorted with electronic clicks.

"Yes. Who's this?" Charlie asked.

"It's"—the line went silent for a moment, then returned—"it's Peter. Can you hear me?"

"Barely," Charlie said.

"—signal is bad in the house," Peter said. "I—warn you."

"Warn me? Warn me about what?" Charlie asked, keeping her voice low but clutching the phone in both hands.

"—see you. I can explain, but—in person. Can—meet up?"

"Meet up? Yeah. I think so. I have to wait until Agent—until my babysitters are asleep. Where do you want to meet?"

"The park—of the street," Peter said. The park at the end of the street, she assumed he meant.

"I don't know when I can get there," Charlie said.

"Come now. Come quickly. You have to—" Peter said, but then the line cut out for good.

Could she afford to wait? It had sounded urgent. She went over to the window. She had, of course, assessed her bedroom window's potential for a secret exit on several occasions, though she'd never had a reason to attempt it. It wasn't like she'd had anything to sneak out to do, or anyone to sneak out to see before. But she knew that if she carefully made her way across the lip of the roof to the oak tree, there was an easy path to climb down.

She checked the outside of the windowsill. There were a couple of little green spiders there, but when she got close to the window, they fled. She closed her hand over the necklace. It must be working.

She glanced over at Miss Sinister. "Is this ridiculous?" she asked. The doll mashed a discarded Post-it note into her wooden jaw and didn't answer.

"No. I'm not going to go meet up with a boy I don't know whose parents are some kind of weird not-person monsters," Charlie told herself. "I'm going to be responsible and sit tight until backup arrives. Right?"

Miss Sinister spat out tiny wet pieces of bright-pink paper. Charlie made a face. How was it *wet* in there?

She didn't want to just sit around waiting for things to go wrong. Maybe Peter could help her. Maybe he *needed* help. He didn't seem like his parents, at least. What if he was in trouble, too?

She nodded to herself. It was the smart thing to do.

She levered up the window, wincing as it creaked. Outside, the air was thick and humid, and the shiver that traveled down her back had nothing to do with the temperature. She listened for any sound of movement in the hall. When there was only silence, she climbed up onto the windowsill, awkwardly working herself out onto the roof while keeping a death grip on the sill. Miss Sinister watched, her beady eyes reflecting the light from outside.

"Miss Sinister, stay," Charlie ordered. She crouch walked her way along the roof, grateful that it wasn't a steep slope, and tried not to look down at just how far she would fall if she slipped.

The oak tree had seemed a lot sturdier for climbing when she was eight, she reflected. The branch that stretched close enough to the roof to reach suddenly looked spindly, and not as close to the house as she remembered. She crouched on the corner of the roof, her throat dry and her hands sweaty. Maybe this had been a bad idea.

A window opening behind her almost made her jump right off the roof. She twisted with a gasp. Gideon hung out of his window, gaping at her.

"What are you doing?" he asked in a loud whisper.

"I'm meeting Peter at the park. He said he had to warn us about something," Charlie whispered back.

"Pendleton and Baxter told us to stay in our rooms," Gideon said.

"I know," Charlie said. "That's why I'm sneaking out."

"But Mom and Dad said they're in charge. We should do what they said," Gideon said fretfully.

"Gideon, they're mind-wobbled. You don't have to do what they say when they're brainwashed," Charlie said patiently. "Go back to bed. You won't get in trouble."

"What if Peter's bad, too? What if it's a trap?" Gideon asked.

"I can take care of myself," Charlie said. And to prove her point, she jumped.

CHAPTER 15

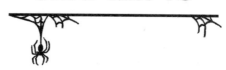

For half a second she was terrified that she had missed and was going to crash straight down to the ground and break an ankle, but then she smacked belly first against the branch, wrapping herself around it. For a moment she hung there like an incompetent sloth, upside down, her cheek pressed against the rough bark. She forced herself to take three quick breaths, then dropped her legs down as she swung from the branch by both hands. Her feet could easily reach the next branch down. She got her balance and eased herself onto it.

From there, it was easy to scramble to the ground, dropping the last few feet to the soft grass with hardly a sound.

She looked up one more time toward Gideon's window. With his light behind him, she couldn't make out his features, but his whole body was tense. She gave him what she hoped was a reassuring wave and sneaked around the front of the house. She kept close to the house at first, ducking under the windows and cutting into the Martins' flower beds. She waited until she was on the far side of the Martins' lawn before she chanced the sidewalk.

Across the street, there was a light on at the Adebayos' house. It was the brothers' bedroom window, judging by the rocket ship curtains. Thomas Adebayo, the younger of the two siblings, was standing there, staring out at the street. Staring at her?

He probably just got up to get a glass of water or something, Charlie thought. She made herself look away and continued toward the park.

She hadn't seen his brother since she'd been in the Weavers' house, it occurred to Charlie.

She hadn't seen the Martins, either.

Any of the houses on the block could be empty, or missing a father or a spouse or a child, and you wouldn't be able to tell. If no one notices you're gone, there's no one to save you, until it's too late.

Was it too late for Mr. Crispin already? She hoped not.

She hoped she hadn't waited too long.

When she arrived at the park, there was no sign of Peter. She sat on one of the swings, the chains creaking as she rocked very gently back and forth. The sky above was clouded, and the air was prickly with the promise of a summer storm. She should be back before it broke, she thought—not because she was afraid, but because Gideon was, and Mom wasn't there to hold him during the thunder.

Matty loved thunder. He liked the feeling of it in his chest. Charlie wasn't afraid of it, but she did find it disconcerting—the way that the rumble and boom seemed to swallow up the sound and sensation of her heartbeat, until it might not be there at all.

As if the storm had filled her rib cage and taken the place of her heart completely. She would put her hand on her chest so she could be sure it was still there.

"Charlie?"

Charlie twisted in her seat. Peter was approaching. He wore a button-up short-sleeve shirt. It was like he was going to church or something. He still had the name tag, now starting to peel off, the sticky edges covered in fuzz and grime.

"Hello, Peter Weaver," she said, as if reading the name tag. He looked down at it and grimaced, then peeled it off, holding it by one corner.

"Your babysitters didn't find out you were in our house, did they?" Peter asked.

"I don't think so," Charlie said. "You didn't tell your parents?"

"Of course not," he said, like this should be obvious. "I wouldn't do that."

They were silent for a moment. Peter shifted his weight; Charlie wondered if she should stand, or say something. Finally, she spoke up. "Why did you want to talk to me?"

Peter glanced away. His fingers moved with nervous energy, folding the name tag in half and then twisting it in his hands. "You know that my parents aren't like normal parents," he said.

"Not normal isn't really the problem," Charlie said. "My family's the furthest thing from normal. What *are* your parents? And don't say a nice, normal couple."

He gave her a hard look. "I don't know if there's a name for what they are. At least not one in a human language. They're not

people. Not exactly. They try to be, but they always get something wrong, so they have to use tricks to fool people. There are
lots of them. Not just my parents. I haven't met most of the others. Mr. Weaver and Mrs. Weaver make me hide when they're
around."

"But what about you? Are you like them?" Charlie asked.

He gave the tiniest shake of his head. "I'm human. At least,
that's what they tell me." His smile was empty and unhappy. "I
think they ate my real parents."

"Ate them?" Charlie asked with alarm. Was that what had
happened to Mr. Crispin?

He nodded glumly. "They feed on people. They move into a
new place, and they trick everyone into seeing what they want
them to see, so no one even notices when they start feeding.
And then when they've had their fill or someone starts to realize
that people are missing, they move on. They all have specialties.
Mr. Weaver and Mrs. Weaver are the Nice Neighbors. There's
one of them—the last time I saw him, he was called Mr. Miller—
he's the New Boss."

Charlie thought of the file. Her mom thought there were
twelve. Hunting in ones and twos and maybe even more, for
decades and decades, and no one had ever even noticed. Except
that Mom had. "But what about you? Why didn't they eat you?"
she asked.

"They use the spiders to make people see what they want—
the venom from the spider bites lets them control people.
But some people are naturally immune to the spiders. Those
people get really bothered by the Weavers. Freaked out. They

can cause problems. But I'm just a person. I can get close to people without making them think there's something wrong with me. Mrs. Weaver thought I might be useful. And Mr. Weaver had promised her she could have a pet," Peter said, his voice thick with bitterness. Charlie shuddered.

"Mr. Crispin could tell there was something wrong with them," Charlie said. She glanced over her shoulder. There was no one in sight, but she got up from the swing and sidled closer to Peter, deeper into the shadows.

"Yeah. That's why they took him first," Peter said. "They've taken a few others, too. The ones they couldn't fool. There's a boy from down the street, and I think some more—I'm not sure."

"Are they dead?" Charlie asked hollowly.

He shook his head. "No. They feed on people for a really long time. That's how they get stronger. They build this big web, and then they capture people and put them in it. It lets them siphon off their captives' extranormal energy a little bit at a time to make themselves more powerful."

Charlie let out a relieved breath. Mr. Crispin and the others—however many there were—could still be saved, then.

He looked miserable. "I don't want to help the Weavers. I swear I don't. But the only times I've tried to get help or to warn people, it's only made things worse."

"But you're warning me," Charlie said softly. He lifted his eyes to hers and nodded slowly. "Why?" she pressed.

Peter wet his lips. "They feed off extranormal energy. Everyone has some, right? Even the most absolutely normal person in the world has a little glimmer. So they can get by taking regular people. But it's like having the same food every day. It gets boring. So sometimes they hunt special people. Extranormal people."

"They fed off of Gideon," Charlie said, remembering the glimmer of light when Mrs. Weaver touched Gideon's forehead and how sick he had become. Disgust curdled in her stomach.

"Psychic ability is like a delicacy," Peter said. "That's why they came here. Because of your family. Because of your mother."

"My mom?" Charlie asked, alarmed. "They want to eat her?"

"She has so much extranormal energy it could feed them for a long, long time. But I don't think it's really about survival. I think it's more like . . . a treat."

"I don't care how good at fooling people they are. My parents will see right through them," Charlie said with a sharp shake of her head.

"That's why we came while your parents were gone," Peter said. "Whenever we come to a new place, it takes a while for the Weavers to get strong enough to start really hunting. It's like building a web—their mind control starts getting stronger and stronger. By the time your parents get here, it'll be strong enough to trap even your mom. Especially with the amber so close by."

Charlie's hand flew to the necklace he'd given her, and his eyes widened.

"Not that amber," he clarified. "That's just a little piece, imbued with some psychic energy. Mrs. Weaver made it for me when she first took me in, so the spiders would stop biting me.

But there's a much bigger amber artifact that works like an amplifier. It makes the Weavers' abilities work way, way better on anyone that's near it. Mr. Weaver said your parents have it."

"Artifact 818," Charlie exclaimed. "But it's in the Malice Vault. It's contained."

"Malice Vault?" Peter asked. Charlie didn't explain. He looked troubled. "When they're near it, they get stronger, and so does the artifact. It's been building up for days. That's why your babysitters got fooled so easily."

Charlie bit her lip. Nothing could get out of the Malice Vault. Could it?

Except that something had, once. All those years ago, something had escaped—enough to open the door. Enough to call her name so sweetly and lure her inside. The Malice Vault was strong. But that didn't mean it was safe.

"Why are you telling me all of this?" Charlie asked.

"Because I don't want you to get hurt," Peter said, looking wounded that she had to ask. "Because I don't want people to get eaten. You should run. Get away from here."

"I already told my parents something is wrong. They'll be coming back. They'll know what to do."

"Don't you get it? That's what the Weavers *want*," Peter moaned. "They're spiders. They make a web and wait for their food to walk into it. With the artifact so close by, they're already strong enough. You have to just get away. Tell your parents not to come."

Charlie knew that wouldn't work. As soon as they knew people were in danger, her parents would charge right in. It was what they did even when their kids *weren't* the ones in mortal peril. "What if we got rid of the artifact?" she asked. "Would they be strong enough then?"

"Maybe. I don't know. I know they thought they were going to need the whole week, before they figured out it was here," Peter said. "What are you thinking?"

"What if we got the artifact out of the house—got it away from everyone? Then the Weavers would be weaker, right?" Charlie asked. Her thoughts were rushing around in her head. She was having trouble holding them all at once, like they were spilling out of her in every direction.

"Charlie, you need to get out of here," Peter said.

"I can't," Charlie said. "Opal can't leave. She's tied to the house." Ghosts were nothing *but* extranormal energy. Opal wouldn't be safe from the Weavers. Maybe she could talk Matty into going, but Gideon wouldn't go with him, not if Charlie wasn't going, and there was no way that Charlie could leave Opal by herself. And then there were Pendleton and Baxter and the Crispin-Suzukis and Martins and Adebayos and everyone else on this street who needed her help.

Hers.

Because she was the only one who knew what was going on. She was the one who had noticed, had figured it out. She couldn't just sit and wait to get rescued, and she couldn't run away. She had to do something. She had to do *this*.

"I'm going to get that artifact," she said, straightening up and setting her jaw. "I'm going to get it out of the house before my parents get here."

"Charlie, the Weavers are too strong. You can't fight them," Peter said. Charlie tipped up her chin, defiant.

"My parents have faced *way* scarier things than the Weavers, and they've beaten all of them," Charlie said, pride making her voice fierce. "I know lots of people who can help. You have no idea. It's all going to be okay, Peter. We'll save everyone— including you."

Instinctively, she reached out and grabbed his hand. He looked startled but didn't pull away. She smiled at him, wild with hope and fear and trying not to show it.

"Trust me, Peter," she said. "We can do this. We're going to get that artifact out of here. And you aren't ever going to have to go back to the Weavers, okay?"

He looked at her as if this was too much to hope for. As if he couldn't even imagine it. "Where else would I go?" he asked, his voice breaking, and her heart broke for him.

"You can stay with us," she said. They had room. Mom and Dad wouldn't hesitate to take him in. This was how all of them had come to be part of the family—lost, orphaned, afraid. Gideon growing up in his cinder block room, surrounded by scientists who poked and prodded at him. Matty a stray on the street, retreating into his wolf to try to be less afraid. Opal, trailing smoke and singeing the carpets, desperately trying to be seen.

Sometimes Charlie felt like she was the least like a Greer of any of them. But they weren't just Greers because of their powers, they were Greers because they were a family who protected people. Took them in. Gave them a home.

She put out her hand. "Come on. We can do this. We'll hide the artifact and get help."

Reluctantly, he nodded. "But how will you get into the vault?" he asked.

"I know the code," she confessed.

"How?" he asked.

"It's a long story, and it doesn't matter now," Charlie said. "We need to hurry, right?"

"Right," he said. His hand was warm, and he held on tight. When she set out, he followed.

CHAPTER 16

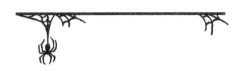

Sneaking out of the house had been pretty easy. Now Charlie realized that she'd never figured out how to sneak back *in*. There were no lights on downstairs, which hopefully meant that the agents were asleep. Charlie brought Peter around to the side door, which made less noise, and used her key to let them inside. She shut the door as softly as she could behind them and then stood there tensely in the dark, waiting for Baxter or Pendleton to loom out of the darkness.

Peter's eyes were wide in the dim light of the clocks and appliances in the kitchen. Charlie took his hand again and slipped out of her shoes, motioning for him to do the same. With their socks making little noise on the floors, they crept into the hall and then up the stairs. She pointed to each step as they went, making sure Peter didn't step on the parts that creaked.

Finally they were at the top. No one stirred. The Weavers didn't seem to be here yet. Good. They had a little time.

"In here," Charlie whispered when they reached the door to the office. The Malice Vault door stood within, as sturdy and seemingly impenetrable as ever.

"That's the vault?" Peter asked, voice hushed. Charlie nodded. He swallowed audibly. "What's in there?"

"Lots of things. None of them good," Charlie said. "It's really important that you not touch anything. Or even look at anything. Stay outside and if you hear anything calling you, even if it sounds like me, don't listen. Unless I say, um, pumpernickel. That's the password, okay?"

"Pumpernickel," he echoed, and didn't question her instructions or look at her like she was out of her mind. She hadn't realized just how much she wished she had someone who would look at her like that. Like he trusted her, and believed her, and didn't think she was strange at all. "Will you be okay?"

"I know how to take care of myself," she said with more confidence than she felt. She'd survived in the Malice Vault once before. This time, she knew what was in there, at least. And the things inside couldn't shut the door anymore, like last time. They couldn't trap her in there.

Still, she didn't move. She stood in front of the Malice Vault and took one deep, steadying breath. And then another. And then another, and now she was getting light headed. Maybe there was such a thing as too much calm breathing.

"You can do this," she told herself. *The first step will be the hardest*, she thought, and forced herself forward. But then the second step turned out to be just as hard.

Memories swarmed in her mind.

Chaaaarlie, the voice had called, the voice that was not her mother's voice. But that wasn't the worst of it. The worst was after the door closed.

The worst was the tender hand running its fingers through her hair with a sound like clicking bones. The worst was the thing in the mirror, pressing its face against the glass and giggling. The worst was the knife asking her to *take me, hold me, use me*, a constant murmur in the back of her mind.

She'd only been inside the vault for two or three minutes. It had felt like a lifetime.

That was why she'd spied on Mom and Dad to learn the code. Not because she wanted to get in—but because she was terrified that someday, despite all Mom's and Dad's reassurances, the things in the Malice Vault would get strong enough to reach out again. Only this time, what if it wasn't Charlie they lured inside? What if it was Opal, or Matty, or Gideon?

What if it swallowed them up, and she couldn't get them out?

Now she put in the code. She'd only seen Mom put it in once, and she'd never tried it to make sure it worked—whenever you put a code in, it got logged by the system, so they would have known she'd done it and changed it.

For a second she feared she'd gotten it wrong, and she couldn't open it after all. But then the light turned green, and the bolts in the door clunked open one by one. Six bolts. Six locks. Charlie put her hand on the handle and pulled.

The door opened.

The lights inside flicked on automatically, and Peter made a startled sound. Charlie remembered flickering, eerie lights, but these were strong and steady. The interior of the room was white and clean, almost antiseptic. There were strips of various kinds of metal set into the floor and the walls—iron and silver, and some others that she didn't know for sure. There were lines of salt, too, contained in grooves, and all kinds of mystical symbols written on the walls.

And as for the occupants of the Malice Vault . . .

Some of the ones she remembered were gone. But the mirror was still there, covered by a blanket. She couldn't hear that eerie giggle, but she thought there was a faint, squeaky scratching, like a sharp nail dragging across glass. The knife was gone, thank goodness. But there was the rocking chair, chained in place so tightly it could hardly move. There was someone in it. Charlie couldn't see them. She couldn't hear them. But she knew. That chair was *not* empty.

She tore her eyes away, fighting the hideous, sickly fear that coated her throat and flooded her belly. She couldn't go in. She had to go in. She had to find Artifact 818.

She took another step. The air shifted almost imperceptibly, and Charlie was overwhelmed with the feeling of being watched.

"Careful," Peter whispered, hanging back.

Her next step took her over the threshold. She could feel something to her left. She could see it out of the corner of her eye, just a gray smudge crouching on top of the armoire there. Blunt fingernails rasped against wood. She didn't look toward it. She knew that if she did, there would be nothing there. She walked forward, staying between the lines of salt and iron and silver. Nothing in the Malice Vault was safe, but this was the safest part of it.

She kept her eyes unfocused as she turned her head slowly to and fro, trying not to actually *look* at any of the objects too closely. Noticing them made them notice you. She let her gaze drift until she saw it. It was sitting on a small pedestal against the left-hand wall, uncomfortably close to the not-empty chair. A chunk of amber, with something dark and spindly suspended within. It had been submerged in a goldfish bowl. Probably salt water, Charlie thought. That was good for making loud things quiet and busy things still.

Next to the goldfish bowl was a small metal box, dull gray with heavy latches. Charlie knew it would be lead lined. It was there in case the artifact needed to be transported. The lead would help keep the psychic field contained, but it also made artifacts angry a lot of the time, so Mom didn't like to leave them stored that way for long. But it would certainly help contain 818 for a little while.

Charlie kept her eyes fixed on the pedestal, not the amber. Whispers and buzzes and vibrations in the air pressed against her skin. She felt like tiny bugs were scampering across her arms and down the back of her shirt, but she knew it was just her imagination.

She couldn't stay here, where it was safe. She had to step past the silver. Past the iron. Past the salt.

Chaaaarlie, a voice whispered, but it was only a memory. Wasn't it?

"Charlie, hurry. They could be on their way right now," Peter urged from the door.

Charlie steeled herself. She could do this. For her family. To prove herself.

She stepped over the three lines in the floor, into the circle that contained the pedestal. Immediately a horrible sound filled her ears, like a whole swarm of cicadas surrounding her. She clapped her hands over her ears, but it did nothing to quiet the noise—it wasn't in the air. It was in her head. She gritted her teeth. The report said the amber made people fall into a stupor, but this was just *loud*.

She plunged her hand into the salt-water-filled fishbowl. The instant her hand closed around the chunk of amber, the sound went completely silent. She felt a delicate sort of pressure against her thoughts, like little legs probing at her. Trying to find a way in. But the amber necklace Peter had given her must be protecting her, because she didn't seem to be affected. She quickly removed the amber and dropped it into the lead-lined box, slopping some salt water in after it for good measure before closing it and throwing the latches shut.

The probing taps against her thoughts stopped. Artifact 818 was silenced, for now. Which meant that she could hear all the other artifacts whispering and murmuring once again.

She bolted for the door. Peter waved her forward, anxiety sketched across his features. She met him at the doorway, holding the lead box aloft.

"I got it," she said. She was shaking so hard the latches rattled.

"Good," Peter said. His voice was calm. Very calm. He'd straightened up, his shoulders no longer hunched. "It will work much better outside the vault."

Charlie froze. "What?"

"We don't really *need* it, but it should make things easier," Peter said. He smiled, and Charlie's stomach sank. "Thank you for getting it. Now give it to me."

"You tricked me," Charlie said, initial horror giving way to embarrassed anger. She'd trusted him. She'd convinced her siblings he was a good guy. Was she really that desperate to have a friend? She glared at Peter, not sure if she was angrier at him or herself. "I was going to help you."

"I don't need help. I have my family," Peter replied.

She stared at him. "You said—but—"

"It doesn't work on everyone, the thing my parents can do," Peter said. "Some people, like me and Mr. Crispin, are resistant. But you—you're completely immune. See, most people have at least a bit of extranormal energy in them. A little bit of luck. A weird talent. So small they might never even find out what it is. But you have nothing. Not one bit of extranormal energy—not one special thing about you. That's why you're immune to the spiders. So the Weavers can't fool you, and there's nothing for them to feed on. So they need you out of the way."

"Is the necklace a trick, too?" Charlie asked.

He shook his head. "I told you the truth. It keeps the spiders from biting you—it just doesn't matter, since you're immune anyway. I gave it to you so you'd like me."

Charlie snarled. She yanked the necklace off and threw it into his face. He barely flinched. The necklace fell to the floor with hardly a sound.

"I'm not giving you the box. And I'm not going to give up," Charlie said. She wrapped her arms around the artifact case. "I won't let them hurt my family."

"You can't stop them," Peter said, shaking his head. "But they don't need you for anything. When they're done, I'll get you, and you can come with us. With me. We can be friends."

She stared at him in horrified confusion. He was smiling. Not the too-wide, too-friendly smile of the Weavers, but a genuine, hopeful smile. Like he really thought there was a possibility that she would agree to go along with his idea.

"I think . . ." Charlie began, as if she was considering the idea. And then she kicked him in the shin as hard as she could.

Peter yelped and staggered back. Charlie charged forward past him. He reached for her arm, his other hand grabbing at his injured leg, but his fingers only raked across her skin. She grabbed the office door, flinging it open—

To find Agent Baxter standing on the other side in flannel pajamas, filling the doorframe. "You're up late, Miss Charlotte," he said.

"Baxter, the Weavers are evil! You have to—" she started, but he reached out and put a hand on her shoulder. A big, firm hand. His fingers dug in under her collarbone, not quite hard enough to hurt. She tried to twist free, but she couldn't get away.

"Miss Charlotte, you're being very rude," Baxter said.

"Put her in the vault," Peter said.

Baxter looked at him with a frown. "I can't do that. It's dangerous," he said.

"I said to put her in the vault. It will keep her safe until all of this is over," Peter said.

"It won't. He's lying. I won't be safe in there," Charlie said, but Baxter was nodding. His hand dropped to her arm, circling it easily. He dragged her toward the open vault door. She threw herself back against his grip, twisting and digging in her heels, but he walked forward as if she weighed no more than a feather.

"Gideon! Opal!" she yelled.

"They can't help you," Peter said. "While we were at the park, your agent friends locked them up. Matty, too."

"If you hurt them—" Charlie started.

"I don't want to hurt them, Charlie. But I can't make any promises about my parents," Peter said, shaking his head sadly. Baxter's face twitched, and for a moment he stood still, his whole body tensing up. She looked at him with a brief flicker of hope—but then he hauled her forward once again and forced her into the vault.

"Get the case. And her phone," Peter said. Baxter nodded. He pried the lead case from Charlie's grasp and reached into her pocket, pulling out her phone. She swiped for it, but she was too slow. Her breath came in quick, panicked gasps and didn't seem to fill her lungs.

"Baxter, please. Don't do this. You have to fight their control. They're evil, they're going to *eat* Mom, you have to—"

"Stay put, Miss Charlotte," Baxter said. And he shut the vault door in her face.

Charlie screamed. She threw herself against the door. She slammed her fists against it, calling for Baxter, for her siblings, for Pendleton—but she knew it was useless. No sound could get through.

She fell back, hands alight with pain from smashing against

the metal again and again. Her throat felt raw. Tears clouded her vision and streaked down her cheeks.

Idiot, she thought. Why had she trusted Peter? She'd thought he was like her siblings. She'd thought all he needed was someone to rescue him. And she'd wanted to be that person. Now she was trapped, and her family was in danger, and there was nothing she could do to help them.

Right at that moment, the lights went out.

CHAPTER 17

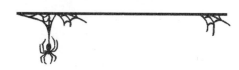

Charlie sat with her back pressed against the door, her arms wrapped around her knees. It didn't matter if her eyes were open or shut; the darkness was the same either way. If there was a switch in the room, she didn't know where. You couldn't open the door from this side at all. She was trapped in here. And she wasn't alone.

Fingernails tapped and scratched against the wood of the armoire beside her. She could *feel* something there, stretching its long body down the side, peering at her. Across the room, chains clinked as the rocking chair shifted ever so slightly. A soft laugh bubbled up from the corner where the mirror stood.

"I'm not afraid of you," Charlie whispered, but she knew nothing and no one believed that. Especially not her.

Of course she was afraid. She remembered what had happened, the last time she was here. Or at least, she remembered pieces of it.

Mostly, she remembered when Mom and Dad burst in. She remembered Dad picking her up and carrying her out in his arms. Later, he told her she was *catatonic*. She had to look up the word. It meant she wasn't moving or talking or doing anything except stare straight ahead.

That was before Mom made all the protections stronger, Charlie reminded herself. She'd be safe as long as she stayed right here. As long as she stayed still.

"*Chaaaarlie*," a voice sighed. Charlie flinched against the cold metal door. "*You came baaaaaack.*"

The thing on the armoire rasped its nails excitedly against the wood. It was right next to her. Six inches away. She could feel its breath against her cheek. It smelled like cedar and damp socks. Charlie dug her fingernails into her legs and bit her lip to keep from crying out. The rocking chair creaked, as if someone had just stood up from it. Footsteps sounded. Whatever it was, it couldn't cross the lines of salt and silver and iron.

Could it?

"*Charlie. Where did you go? You were gone for so long,*" a voice sang. Charlie didn't hear it so much as she *felt* it, inside her mind.

Don't talk to them, Charlie told herself. Don't acknowledge them. Don't react.

"*We won't hurt you, Charlie. We can't hurt you. We don't want to hurt you,*" the voice sang sweetly, and then laughed. The thing on the wardrobe made a wet clicking sound in the back of its throat.

Don't talk to them, don't look at them, don't think about them, Charlie told herself.

"*You left us all alone, Charlie. After we became such good friends,*" the voice whispered in her mind. There was a faint glow at the end of the room. Spilling out from under the blanket that covered the mirror.

"Don't you remember us? We remember you. We remember the hours we spent together in the dark."

Charlie stiffened. She hadn't been in here for hours. The voice was lying.

"Charlie, Charlie, Charlie," the voice sang in her mind. *"We called and you came. The door was open, and you walked through, and we closed it behind you. A little bit of mischief. And we were cruel, oh, and hungry, oh, and hateful, and you have your mother's eyes, Charlotte Greer, and we wanted to pluck them out."*

"But you didn't," Charlie said, voice shaking. The door had barely been shut for a few minutes when her mother and her father got her out.

Right?

"They weren't here, Charlie. They weren't here to protect you. The old woman they left to care for you was our appetizer. We ate her up and left nothing but an echo of a scream, and then we called to you, and you came, such a good girl, such an obedient girl. We wanted to eat you, too, but we couldn't."

Charlie rose. Her mouth was dry. Her heart was pounding. The light under the blanket pulsed and shimmered, and she walked toward it. She knew she shouldn't. She knew she should sit still and hope for rescue. But a memory was wriggling like a worm in her mind. A memory not of minutes but of hours in the dark. Of a woman—Mrs. Lancaster, wasn't that her name?—and a single narrow shoe, discarded in the middle of the vault.

Mrs. Lancaster. She'd been older. Gray hair, thin lips. Not mean, but not warm and friendly, either. She had been unimpressed with the suggestion of the extranormal. Hokum and nonsense, she'd called it, but Dad called her *reliable* and more importantly *available*. Charlie had never thought to wonder why Mrs. Lancaster stopped babysitting her when Mom and Dad were away. She'd never connected it to that night.

Charlie approached the mirror. She knew she shouldn't. She knew how foolish it was. But she reached out to grab the blanket. Because she knew what was under there. She remembered—or she almost did. And she had to see it again.

She pulled. The blanket came away easily, as if it had only been waiting for permission to fall. Charlie stared into the glass, lit with an eerie glow. There was no reflection. Only mist—and a hand pressed against the other side of the glass.

"Charlie."

She'd been so little. It was before even Matty arrived. Six years old and so, so scared. In the dark, all alone.

Except not alone.

Because she'd had a friend.

She put her hand to the glass. Palm to palm with the person on the other side.

Out of the mist stepped a girl. She looked almost like Charlie. Or like she was *supposed* to look like Charlie but had taken a wrong turn somewhere along the way. She had the same red hair and the same blue eyes, but her face was narrower, and her nose was smaller, and there was a sharpness to her features that made her look like a weasel or a fox. Something that ate small helpless creatures, snatching them up with a quick bite of the jaws.

"Who are you?" Charlie asked.

"I should be you," the girl replied. Her voice was real now, not just in Charlie's head.

"But you're not."

The girl shook her head, a curl of a smile in the corner of her mouth. "You don't have what we need. You look like a tasty little morsel, but there's nothing to eat," she said. "We are always, always hungry. But you are completely unappetizing."

Charlie felt queasy. "Because I'm not special."

"Not at all. Not *even* a little bit. Not even enough to fill the tiniest toe!" the girl said, and laughed, clapping her hands. "Isn't it funny? Isn't it hilarious? Isn't it wonderful? You're dull as dirt. Duller! So we can't eat you."

"You can't hurt me?" Charlie asked.

She *tsked* and shook her head. "I said we can't *eat* you. We can hurt you plenty, plenty, plenty. But don't worry. I don't want to. And I won't let the others hurt you, either. I like you. We're friends." Her smile was strange, like there were other rows of teeth behind it. Rows and rows and rows.

"You were in here with me that night," Charlie said.

The girl nodded. "At first we were just playing with our food. Then we realized you weren't a snack at all, and the others were going to kill you, but I said no."

"Why?" Charlie asked. Was there something *good* in the girl in the mirror? Was it a mistake, that she was in the Malice Vault?

"I don't know. It's boring in here. You were something different, at least," the girl said, and flicked her hair over her shoulder. "We played. We played lots of games." She grinned a grin that showed off those extra rows of teeth, and Charlie stumbled back, suddenly glad she couldn't remember much about that night. "Will you play with me again, Charlie?"

"I have to get out of here," Charlie said.

"No, no, no. Don't go, go, go. You belong in here with us now," she said brightly. She pressed both palms against the glass. "Play with us, Charlie. Play!"

The girl slammed her hands against the glass. It began to bow outward, and Charlie yelped, scrambling back—over the line of salt, the line of iron, the line of silver. The girl howled and slammed against the glass again and again. The rocking chair began to strain frantically against its chains. The thing on the wardrobe gibbered and scrabbled up one side and down the other and back again, and in the shadows, something chattered its teeth.

"Play with us, Charlie. What fun we had! The drowning game was the best. And the game of skin! Don't you remember that one?"

Charlie sank down to the ground, closing her eyes and covering her ears.

She remembered cold water.

She remembered thick, suffocating cloth all around her, holding her still.

She remembered twisted shapes that shouldn't have existed, and how they moved with jerky steps and gasping breaths.

She remembered her mother's hand against her cheek. *Oh, my love. You're safe now. Let's send those shadows away.*

Her mother had Soothed her, she realized. Leigh Greer had touched a hand to her face and locked up all those horrid memories like discarded toys in the back of the closet, but they were still there.

"That salt and iron and silver won't hold us back for long. Not with you in here, keeping us awake," the girl in the mirror taunted.

Charlie sobbed, tears running down her cheeks. She didn't have her mother's gift. Or any gift at all that could be useful. The only reason she'd survived was that she was *nothing* to these monsters, and now she was stuck in here with them again.

But she *had* survived. She'd gotten out.

She would get out again.

She told herself not to be afraid. But that was impossible. So be afraid, she thought, and survive anyway. Her mother had her gift to rely on, to keep her alive. But Dad didn't. How did Dad survive all the things they'd fought? She tried to picture his face.

The first thing you have to do is understand what you're up against.

Sometimes they were dealing with a person. Sometimes it was a monster or a spirit or a spell. But whatever it was, the first thing to know was what it *wanted*. Its intent. Did it want revenge? Was it hungry? And if it was hungry, what was it hungry *for*? Some things fed on fear, so you had to let go of fear. Some things fed on certain kinds of people, or during certain times.

The things in here were dangerous in part because they were *always* hungry, and they would feed on anything—anything except her, apparently. But they still would delight in tormenting her. Even killing her.

What did she know about the things in the Malice Vault? Most of them were quiet right now; they were less active, less *awake*. She didn't think she needed to do anything but stay away from them. The girl in the mirror, though, was another matter. Charlie tried to remember what her parents had told her about the mirror.

It made itself look like you, trapped you inside, and took your place. She hadn't been able to copy Charlie, but Charlie was pretty sure she had pulled her inside the mirror anyway. Which meant she could do it again.

But maybe Charlie could give the mirror girl something else to copy.

The thing on the wardrobe. For most people, it didn't look like anything more than a smudge at the corner of your vision, and it disappeared if you looked right at it. But Mom could see it. She said it was an old woman who crouched up there in a nightgown, her knees sticking up above her head, her cracked and yellowed fingernails scratching and tapping. The only time people saw her, actually saw her, was when she dropped down and stuck her face in theirs and then—

Well, Charlie didn't know *exactly* what happened after that. She just knew that Mom and Dad wouldn't tell her, which must mean it was really bad. *If you see her face, it's the last thing you see.*

That gave her an idea. The girl in the mirror had fallen silent.

Bored, maybe. Charlie stood up. The girl was gone, though the glow and the roiling mist remained. Charlie picked up the blanket from where it had puddled on the ground.

"What are you doing, Charlie?" the girl in the mirror asked, starting to emerge from the mist.

Charlie quickly threw the blanket over the mirror, blocking out the sight of the girl. The light in the room instantly dimmed; Charlie could barely even see right in front of herself.

The girl laughed. "That won't stop me for long, Charlie," she said.

Charlie clenched her back teeth together, shutting out the sound of the girl's voice. She walked around behind the mirror. It was heavy, but not so heavy that she couldn't budge it. Careful to only touch the parts wrapped in the blanket, she started pushing and wiggling it across the floor. It scraped and screeched. When she shoved it across the protective lines, the girl gave a yelp, and another laugh.

"Are you letting me out, Charlie? Do you think I'll spare you if you do?" she asked. Charlie didn't answer. She was halfway across the room. Three-quarters of the way. The mirror seemed to hum beneath her hands, making the bones in her fingers and wrists ache. The blanket rippled. The girl clapped.

Almost there. Charlie stepped around the mirror to the front, keeping her eyes fixed on her feet. She dragged it another few inches, stepping backward.

"I can feel you there. You can't hide from me. Oh, this is fun," the girl said.

Behind Charlie wood creaked. Two hands settled on her

shoulders. She couldn't see them, but she could feel the soft, powdery skin. The rough, cracked fingernails. A hot breath gusted against her cheek as long hair dragged across her upper arms, and the thing from the wardrobe let out a moan of anticipation. Terror thundered through Charlie, but she held her scream behind clamped lips. Across the room, the rocking chair strained back and forth as if in excitement.

"Charlie, you—" the girl in the mirror began.

Charlie grabbed the blanket in both fists and yanked, throwing herself to the side in the same instant. She saw in her mind what would happen: the blanket would fall away. The girl in the mirror would see the thing on the wardrobe, and they would leap at each other—

But the blanket caught. Instead of falling away from the mirror, it snagged, and sent Charlie toppling, twisting to land in an ungainly heap. She pushed herself up—and realized she was staring straight at the wardrobe.

At the withered old woman in the moth-eaten nightgown who clung to it upside down like some horrible, bent-legged spider, her jaw gaping and the sockets of her eyes empty except for the fluttering, dusty wings of moths. Her fingernails were yellow and thickly ridged as she reached her hands toward Charlie's face. Charlie tried to scream or run, but she was frozen as terror locked up her joints.

The woman's hands cupped the sides of her face, and her mouth stretched wide.

Charlie felt something *tugging* deep within her, and with it came a sense of overwhelming hunger—the old woman's hunger. She was feeding on Charlie.

Trying to feed.

The girl in the mirror had said there was nothing there to feed on. But that wasn't quite it. The woman's dark energy reached into Charlie's soul—and it was like dropping a dried-out sponge into a shallow puddle of water. All that dark energy rushed into Charlie and pulled out of the old woman so fast that neither one of them had time to react, except for a quick, cut off scream that sounded as dusty as the moth wings—and then the old woman crumbled.

Literally crumbled. Her skin dried up. Her limbs pulled inward like a dead bug, and she fell off the wardrobe with a thump and a rattle of bones and a puff of dust, and then there was nothing left of her except a big pile of what looked like fireplace ash and a few moths struggling weakly through it.

Charlie gaped. She could feel the woman's dark energy still roiling inside her, but it was vanishing quickly. Drying up as rapidly as it had rushed in, like it couldn't exist inside her.

The Malice Vault was silent. The chair had stopped rocking. The girl in the mirror didn't make a sound.

Charlie stood up slowly. She reached up and pulled off the blanket. The girl was standing very still, looking like someone who had been caught in a very big lie and was not yet sure if they're about to get in trouble.

"What just happened?" Charlie asked, anger and uncertainty making her voice rough. The girl shimmered—and disappeared. She was gone.

Charlie couldn't feel the dark energy inside her anymore, like it had all soaked in and vanished. She thought of the little packets that sometimes came in packages and shoeboxes and things. The ones that said DO NOT EAT and soaked up all the moisture in the box so things stayed dry. A desiccant, she remembered, and wasn't quite sure why she'd thought of it.

A memory stirred, long buried. She remembered the feel of a knife in her hands. *The* knife, *drip*, *drip*, *dripping* with blood. It had whispered in her head. Called to her. But she hadn't wanted to do what it said.

She didn't remember what had happened next. But she had the faint memory of chalky ash on her fingers, and one last blackened chunk of the blade plinking to the floor.

"What's happening?" she whispered. But the room was suddenly perfectly quiet.

CHAPTER 18

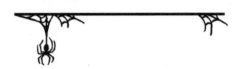

In the dark, in the silence, Charlie waited. Her stomach growled. Her eyelids dragged with weariness. She forced them to stay open. Forced herself to stay awake. She had to be wary. The girl in the mirror had gone quiet and sulky under the blanket, and nothing else had moved, but if she let her guard down, she knew they'd try to come for her.

She wasn't sure exactly how long she'd been here. Hours, definitely. Long enough to be ravenously hungry and completely exhausted. The seconds and minutes blurred together and collapsed until everything felt like one big smear of time. Was it morning? Afternoon? She couldn't tell. She pinched at her arms to keep herself awake and stared into the dark, watching for any flicker of movement that might signal danger.

She let herself hope for rescue. But only a little. Any more than that, and it started to hurt.

So when a sound broke the quiet of the vault, it wasn't hope that she felt first, but fear. The sound was echoing and metallic, and it was coming from right down by the floor on an empty patch of wall. Heart thumping, Charlie crept toward it.

Lit faintly by the mirror's glow was an air vent, covered with a grate. And behind the grate was a familiar doll in voluminous black petticoats.

"Miss Sinister!"

Charlie had never been so happy to see the cursed doll. She dropped down to her knees and lowered her face to look at the doll, who growled grumpily.

"Miss Sinister, are you okay?" Charlie asked. She tried to reach a finger through the grate, but the openings were too thin. Miss Sinister touched a wooden hand against the very tip of her finger and clacked her mouth angrily. "They didn't hurt you, did they?"

The doll shook herself and growled again. Charlie wasn't sure if that was an answer, but she didn't seem to be any worse for wear, at least. She wished she could ask Miss Sinister what was going on—but as clever as the doll could be at times, she wasn't smart enough to answer.

But she might be smart enough to help.

Charlie peered into the air vent. It was barely big enough for Miss Sinister to fit inside—certainly far too small for a person. But maybe Miss Sinister could carry a message? Except she couldn't talk, and the only pen and paper in the vault would almost certainly be fatal to use (it was locked in the old-fashioned desk on the other side of the room and had claimed the lives of multiple poets). She wasn't confident enough in her newfound ability—or extreme lack of ability?—to take that kind of risk.

She ran her fingers along the edge of the vent grate. It was secured in place with four screws at the corners. There was no way to fit a screwdriver through the slot, but maybe . . . "Miss Sinister, I need your help. I need you to listen to me and try to understand, okay?"

Miss Sinister clacked her jaw once, her eyes glowing intently and fixed on Charlie. Charlie hoped that meant she understood. "Okay. I need you to go to my room. My library card is on the desk. Get it and bring it here." The library card should be sturdy enough that she could use the corner to unscrew the grate. Then once it was open, Miss Sinister could bring her a phone.

But one thing at a time. She didn't want to confuse the doll.

Miss Sinister scuttled backward, receding from view until only her glowing eyes showed, and then she turned a corner and vanished. Charlie sat up, rubbing her arms. Had Miss Sinister understood? Would she do what she was told?

It could go either way on both counts. All Charlie could do was wait.

To her relief, she didn't need to wait long. After only a couple of minutes, Miss Sinister clattered her way back to the grate and quickly fed something through the gap. Charlie took it eagerly—and then sighed as she looked down at the corner-store receipt she now held. $3.13 for a candy bar and a root beer.

"No, not this. The library card. On my desk," Charlie said. She held up her fingers in the shape of the card. Miss Sinister growled. Charlie thought furiously. "It looks like the credit card? That Mom uses to order pizza?" At the word *pizza*, Miss Sinister perked up. She had a penchant for anchovies. She didn't eat them—she just hid them under furniture.

Miss Sinister made an excited noise.

"No, we're not getting pizza. The card, get the card," Charlie said, covering her face with one hand and groaning. Skittering and rustling told her that Miss Sinister had taken off again. "Please, please, please," Charlie chanted to herself. She had never once wished that Miss Sinister was smarter, before this moment. She was plenty of trouble as it was, her viciousness constrained by her limited intelligence.

Now, though, Charlie could really use an evil genius.

Twenty minutes later, Charlie sat in front of a pile of index cards, bookmarks, candy wrappers, receipts, and string. On the other side of the grate were larger items that couldn't fit through—a rubber bouncy ball, a box for a video game, various pens and pencils, and a chopstick that, judging by the amount of dust on it, had probably been lost behind the fridge. Charlie's shoulders were slumped. Her mouth was uncomfortably dry, and she wished she could get Miss Sinister to bring her a water bottle and a straw to feed through the vent so she could drink it. But they were still working on the library card.

The now-familiar metallic skittering filled the vent, and Miss Sinister popped into view. "What do you have this time?" Charlie asked wearily.

Miss Sinister shoved her prize through the vent. Charlie stared.

It was a library card.

It wasn't *her* library card. It was Gideon's—but it was stiff plastic, and the corner was just the right size, and she didn't care whose it was.

"You are amazing. Perfect. Magnificent!" Charlie told the doll. Miss Sinister preened as best as a cursed, dust-covered granny doll could.

Charlie wiped relieved tears from her eyes and slotted the corner of the card into the screw at the top right of the grate. It wasn't perfect—the plastic had more bend to it than she would have liked, and it didn't fit exactly—but she managed to get the screw moving. Soon it was loose enough that she could start twisting it with her fingers, and less than a minute later it plinked onto the floor.

"Three more to go," Charlie said. She considered. This was going to take a little while. And so was getting anything else useful from Miss Sinister. "Miss Sinister, I need my phone. You know what a phone is, right?"

Miss Sinister clattered her limbs against the floor of the vent, then sped off. Charlie sighed and wondered what she'd come back with.

She started on the next screw.

She wasn't sure how long it all took, exactly, except that by the time she got the third screw out and was able to rotate the vent out of the way, she could barely see Miss Sinister behind the wall of random objects she'd accumulated.

"Well, at least we found the remote," Charlie said, plucking it out of the pile. It had been missing for weeks. And behind it . . . "You got it! Good job," Charlie said, snatching up her phone. Miss Sinister scrambled over the pile of other junk and crouched on the ground, looking around the Malice Vault with narrowed eyes.

Charlie ignored her and focused on the phone. It didn't have much battery left—5 percent. She'd have to work fast. She opened up her text messages and frowned. There were a bunch of messages from her that she hadn't sent—to AD Dixon, and Mom, and Dad, and even the Operative, telling all of them that nothing was wrong and not to worry. Had Pendleton and Baxter sent them? Or maybe Peter. They didn't read like her, but she didn't expect an adult to notice that.

There was a voicemail message, too. From Dad. She pressed play and held the phone up to her ear.

"Charlie, it's Dad. We got your message. I don't know what's going on there, but Dixon said you've been asking some pretty strange questions. Pendleton and Baxter say there's nothing wrong, but I'm going to be honest, they seemed off. We're heading back right away. And in the meantime, Dixon's going to swing by. Hang tight and call me when you can, okay?"

A wave of relief washed over Charlie—followed by a surge of panic. She jammed the call button and listened to the ringing— but it went straight to voicemail.

"Dad! You can't come back. It's a trap! The Weavers want to eat Mom." She babbled as much as she could before the message cut her off. Then she tried Mom's phone. That one went to voicemail, too—did that mean they were on a plane already?

Her phone battery was down to 4 percent. She took a deep breath. She couldn't help anyone from in here. She needed to get out.

Opal and Gideon didn't have phones—they were too young, plus Opal couldn't use one and Gideon tended to make complicated electronics short out when he got stressed, which was basically all the time. But Matty had a phone.

Except . . .

She stared at the time on the phone. It was 7:00 p.m. No wonder she was starving and thirsty. She'd been in here for almost an entire day. It was Sunday evening, and that meant that Matty was locked in the basement. She groaned. He wouldn't have transformed yet, but the basement was super secure. It didn't have a vent for Miss Sinister to scurry through, even, and Matty wasn't allowed to bring his phone, since anything that was in there needed to be completely chew proof once the sun set.

"Miss Sinister, I need you to listen *very carefully*," Charlie said. The doll looked at her with rapt attention. Charlie searched for signs of intelligence behind her eyes and got only the impression of an empty hallway and the distant tones of a doorbell. She sighed. They'd gotten this far. She'd just have to have faith. "Get Matty's phone. Bring it to Gideon." Simple words. Simple mission. "Bring Matty's phone to Gideon," she repeated.

The doll set out. Charlie fired off a quick text, so it would be on the screen when Gideon—hopefully—got the phone.

> Trapped in the Malice Vault. Battery running out.
> Text when you have phone.

Then she waited. And waited. And waited. Her battery ticked down to 3 percent. She made herself stop turning on the screen to check it. It was only wasting more battery. She shut her eyes and bit the inside of her cheek, praying for her phone to chime.

And chime it did.

She looked down at the screen, letting out a shuddering breath of relief.

Baxter and Pendleton locked me in my room
They put salt around Opal's room
so she's stuck too
Matty's locked in the basement
What's going on?

They're after Mom
The Weavers are
Too long to explain.
I need you to get me out

I'm locked in

Unlock your door!
Like you did with the filing cabinet.

Pendleton and Baxter told me to stay

They're mind-wobbled!

What if you're wrong?
I don't want to get in trouble

Charlie pinched the bridge of her nose. She wanted to yell at him. She wanted to shake him. But he wasn't here, and anyway, that would only make him shut down. It wasn't his fault he was so afraid to break rules all the time. It was the fault of the people who had made him, and hurt him. She was mad at *them*. Gideon didn't need mad. He needed gentle. He needed love.

And the Greers had so much love.

Gideon, you are going to have to be brave.
I know that it's scary, but I know you can do it.
You don't think you're brave but you are.
So, so brave. You always have been.
You had to start a whole new life when
you left the facility.
You had to figure out how a whole
new world worked.
And look at you!
You are sweet and smart and funny.
You are such a good brother to Opal.
And to me and Matty.
We are so lucky Mom and Dad brought you home.
We are so lucky to be your family.
And right now, we're lucky because you are
exactly the person we need.

You are the one that can help your family.

Because nobody else could get out of that room.

But you can.

You can help me.

We can help Mom.

We CAN.

YOU can.

Please.

There was a long, long silence. The screen went dark. And then—

Okay.

Charlie let out a sob of relief.

Good. You need to unlock your door and then come get me out.

I can't. Baxter is in the office. Pendleton left. I don't know where to.

Charlie rubbed her forehead. Gideon wouldn't be able to get past Baxter on his own. They'd have to draw him away, but how? It couldn't just be Gideon. They'd need Opal, too. And they needed to make sure Baxter wouldn't be able to just throw them all in the Malice Vault again.

But Gideon couldn't stand up to authority figures. Opal

panicked. Matty wouldn't follow directions. This was never going to work. She wasn't there to help.

Which meant she was going to have to trust them, she realized. She had to trust that they could do what they had to. That they were strong enough—even without her.

> I think I have a plan, but it means you're going to have to be very brave.
> You and Matty and Opal.
> I won't be able to help you.
> You have to do it on your own.

Silence again. Charlie chewed her lip. Finally the answer came through.

> What do you want us to do?

> First, you're going to pick the lock on your door.
> Get Opal's door open and break the salt line so she can cross.
> I know that you're scared of getting in trouble, but you need to do it.
> Then Opal is going to have to distract Agent Baxter.
> I know that she's going to be scared, too.
> You have to tell her to be brave, and be fierce, and not disappear.
> Because she has to keep Baxter's attention. Even

if it means hurting him a little bit.

Because while she's distracting him, you're going to go to the basement and unlock Matty's door.

Here's the important part. Matty can't leave yet. And he's not going to like this, but he has to hide. He has to be very patient and wait for the right moment, not charge in. Because Opal is going to lead Baxter down to the basement, and then disappear.

He'll see that the door is open.

Use your powers to make it sound like Matty is still in there. Baxter will have to investigate.

As soon as he's inside, you and Matty slam the door shut and lock it.

Then you come get me out. The code is 851923-451978.

Do you understand?

At that moment, the phone shut down. The battery was dead. She had no way to talk to Gideon. No confirmation beyond that single *okay* that he could actually do this. He was only eight. He was scared, and he hated breaking the rules, and he'd only done the lock-picking thing once, on a different kind of lock. Opal was terrified. Would she even be there when Gideon got past the salt, or would she have retreated back into her own world?

Would she be able to be fierce and bold enough to distract Baxter? Would Matty be able to restrain himself from charging in long enough to fool the agent?

She couldn't do anything. She couldn't help them. She couldn't do it herself. She just had to wait. Wait and hope.

Wait and trust.

She spent so much time thinking about her sibling's problems that she didn't take a lot of time to think about what they were good at.

They were special, sure. But it was more than that. They were *amazing*. Gideon had been so sweet and careful with that butterfly. It had taken him all his concentration and given him a migraine for three days, and he hadn't even cared, he was so proud. Who else would be that kind to a butterfly?

And Opal. Back in San Francisco, she'd tried again and again to get people to see her and hear her. She'd never given up on people. Lots of ghosts got angry and bitter, cut off from their humanity, but she was still the same loving little girl she had been in life. She fought so hard to hold on to herself, to hold on to her family, that she was getting more and more real, instead of less.

And Matty . . . Charlie felt a flicker of irritation, thinking of how stubborn he was, how annoying, but she balled up her fists. If this didn't work and she got stuck in here forever or sucked into a mirror, she wanted her last thoughts about her family to be good ones. And there were so many good things about Matty. Like how resourceful he was. And he was really good at making friends, which she sure wasn't. Plus, sometimes you needed someone to be a bit reckless. Life was more fun that way.

He'd covered for her when she sneaked out to the Weavers'

house, hadn't he? And he'd believed her when she told him there was something wrong. Even if he didn't understand it at first. Maybe they didn't always get along, but he was her brother, and they loved each other. They were loyal to each other.

We're each other's pack, she thought, and smiled to herself.

More than anything, she wished Matty was here right now. He wouldn't have sat around moping and scared like she had. He would have come up with a plan. Eight plans.

They'd probably also have gotten eaten by something when those plans didn't work, of course.

But at least she wouldn't have been eaten alone.

Trust wasn't just something that *happened*, she realized. It was something you had to choose. She had to choose to trust her siblings—even if it meant they didn't need her after all.

She waited. And hoped. And waited. She swung wildly between being certain that Gideon would panic and wouldn't leave his room, that he was about to open the door and save her—and then back again, around and around. Thinking of all the ways her plan could fail. That her siblings could fail.

Until finally, the keypad beeped. The locks on the door clunked open one by one. Charlie was on her feet and running toward the door before she even registered the noise, and then it swung open, revealing Gideon and Matty and Opal and a very smug-looking Miss Sinister.

Charlie wanted to shout for joy, but she kept quiet as she threw herself out of the room and shut the door quickly—and quietly—behind her. She collapsed against it, barely keeping her feet under her, and grinned at her siblings.

"You did it," she said in a whisper, her hands shaking too much to sign.

Gideon's face was ashen with stress, but he nodded. "Baxter almost saw me when I left my room."

Opal hovered nervously, thick smoke coiling around her. "I had to burn him. A little bit. I didn't want to. Just on his arm, a little," she said, then wrapped her arms around herself.

"She was awesome," Matty said. "I just hid under a chair. It took forever for her to get him down in the basement. I wanted to bite him." He wrinkled his lip, baring teeth that were looking a little sharper than usual. His eyes were bright yellow. Charlie glanced at the clock on the wall. Not long left before he would transform.

"It was really, really, really scary," Opal said.

"But you did it," Charlie told her. She smiled at all of them. "All of you did something that was hard for you, and you did it perfectly. Baxter won't be able to get out of the basement. But where's Pendleton?"

"He said something about the airport?" Gideon said, uncertainty turning it into a question. Charlie's stomach flipped. Pendleton was picking Mom and Dad up at the airport? But surely they'd check their phones and see that he couldn't be trusted.

"Is something going to happen to them?" Opal asked fretfully.

"No. We won't let anything happen to them," Charlie said. "But we don't know what the Weavers have planned. We have to handle the Weavers before Mom and Dad get here. Which means we have to act fast, and we have to be smart. Dad said that Assistant Director Dixon was coming. Have you seen him?"

Gideon blanched and nodded. "He was across the street. Talking to the Weavers. He went inside and then he came back out and got in the car with Pendleton."

Charlie hissed between her teeth. Mom and Dad knew that they couldn't trust Pendleton, but Dixon was another matter. They might not realize he was mind-wobbled. "Give me Matty's phone. And go plug mine in, will you?"

Matty gave Gideon a nod, and he handed Charlie the phone, trading for hers, which he plugged in to charge on Mom's desk. Charlie called Dad's number. It went straight to voicemail.

"They got to Dixon, too. You can't trust anyone," she said, and then dialed Mom's number. To her relief, the line picked up—and then her heart sank as Pendleton answered.

"Hello, Charlie," he said. "I assume it's Charlie."

"Where are my parents?" Charlie demanded.

"Oh, they're on their way home," Pendleton said. "They should be there soon. Assistant Director Dixon is giving them a lift."

"You need to snap out of it, Pendleton! You know this isn't right!" Charlie shouted into the phone.

"I don't—I can't—" Pendleton said. "Charlie . . ."

He hung up. Charlie snarled at the phone and practically threw it at Matty. "They're on their way from the airport." Pendleton hadn't said whether they were already on their way or heading for the car, but if he had Mom's phone, they'd gotten off the plane, that much she could tell. There were two airports nearby—one of them would take at least an hour, but the other one was only half the time. Unless there was traffic.

They'd have to pray for traffic.

"Think," Charlie told her siblings. "How do we stop the Weavers?"

"Kill them," Matty suggested, teeth bared.

Charlie gave him a flat look. "Let's hold that in reserve. They might be monsters, but I don't think Mom and Dad would like us killing anything."

"They're spiders. Nothing wrong with smashing spiders," Matty insisted.

"Spiders are very important and helpful," Gideon objected.

"Fine. Then we trap them under a giant glass and take them outside," Matty said, rolling his eyes.

"How would we even kill them?" Gideon asked. "Are you going to eat them? You're the size of a corgi when you transform."

"I'm bigger than a corgi," Matty said, offended.

"Peter said that they feed on people to make themselves stronger," Charlie said. "He said that they have a big web that lets them hold people and siphon off their energy. We need to find out where Mr. Crispin and the others are. If we save them and destroy the web, we cut off the Weavers' source of food. Then they'll be weak."

"Maybe weak enough that they can't mind-wobble people. Then we wouldn't have to fight them on our own," Gideon said.

Matty looked thoughtful. "Where would they be keeping people? At the house?"

"When I was in there, I didn't see any sign of Mr. Crispin," Charlie said.

"What about the basement?" Matty suggested.

"Do they have a basement?" Charlie asked. She hadn't seen a door that could have led to one.

"Mrs. Stanton definitely had a basement," Matty said. "I went down there once to get her a jar of olives. It had been expired since before I was born." He shuddered theatrically. "The door is in the kitchen."

Charlie closed her eyes, trying to picture the kitchen. She remembered the fridge, the busted stove, the discolored walls—and a cabinet standing against one wall. "I think they hid it," she said.

"Which definitely means there's something down there," Matty replied.

It made sense. When Peter had helped her sneak out of the house, his parents hadn't been in sight, and she should have been able to see them, or at least hear them, from the foyer.

Peter. Her fingers curled tightly into fists. She should never have trusted him. She'd *liked* him. And he'd been tricking her all along. She felt like a fool. Tears of humiliation blurred her vision.

Something bumped against the side of her hand. She looked down to find Opal, brow knit, brushing the side of Charlie's hand with her own. The slightest point of contact.

"Charlie, don't be sad," Opal said. "We're together. And Greers can do anything together. Right?"

Charlie nodded, sniffling. They were together, and that was what mattered. And they didn't have time for her to break down.

She looked around at each of them. "What should we do?" she asked. "What do *you* think we should do?"

They blinked. "Shouldn't you decide? You're the oldest," Gideon said.

"Technically, Opal's the oldest," Matty countered. Opal squeaked and immediately sank several inches into the floor.

Charlie looked around at them. "You got me out of the Malice Vault. You're all smart, and you've got powers that mean you see and think about things differently. What would you do, if you had to do this by yourself?" Charlie asked.

"Hide," Opal said. "Hide until it's all over."

"Bite them," Matty said, fingers like fangs.

"Get help," Gideon said.

"But who could help us? Dixon came, and he just got mind controlled," Matty said. "The last thing we need is them to mind control the Operative or something."

Charlie snapped her fingers. "The Operative!"

"He would probably get mind-wobbled and blow us up," Matty said.

"I don't mean we get the actual Operative. He's probably still in France anyway," Charlie said. "But he sent Opal a doll for her birthday."

"How is a doll going to help us?" Gideon asked.

"I mentioned it the other day and he acted really weird about it, so I started thinking. I mean, come on. The Operative? Sent a doll?" Charlie repeated, and Gideon, Matty, and Opal all widened their eyes.

"It's gotta be a weapon," Matty said.

They scrambled out the door together and piled into Opal's room. The doll had been relegated to the little wooden chair in the corner of the room, where Opal placed her less favored possessions. It was no surprise she hadn't decided to give this one a place of honor on the bed—it looked like an off-brand Raggedy Ann doll, with purplish yarn hair and a lumpy torso stuffed into a gingham dress. Matty descended on the doll, flipping it over and tearing at the seams on the back with enthusiasm and no small bit of snarling.

"That's my doll!" Opal objected.

"We'll get you a new one," Charlie said reassuringly. Opal huffed but nodded. The seam tore. Matty reached into the cavity and pulled out a fistful of stuffing—along with a long, pale rod of what looked like crystal.

"Is that . . ." Gideon started.

"Alien crystal," Charlie said. "The kind that goes boom."

"And Dad thought he was finally catching on," Gideon said sadly, shaking his head.

"We probably should have been way more suspicious," Charlie said, though she was rather glad they hadn't.

Matty reached inside again and extracted a silvery metal plate about the size of a credit card, with little blue gems on the side. Charlie tried to think back to the Operative's lessons, that day he took her out for ice cream. Mostly she remembered that he'd let her get a waffle cone and as many toppings as she wanted, but she seemed to recall that you had to attach the control plate to the crystal to activate it. And then you had to get away—*fast*.

"We were sleeping with that in the house?" Opal asked, voice squeaky with alarm.

"Not like it would have hurt *you*," Matty reminded her.

"It's totally harmless on its own. You can chuck it in a fire and nothing will happen. You need the control card to make it do anything," Charlie said, showing them the metal plate.

"Should we be worried that you know that?" Gideon asked.

Charlie took the crystal gingerly from Matty. "I've known the Operative my whole life, and we weren't *always* supervised. I've picked up a few things. Don't tell Dad. Anyway, if we can get this into the basement, we can set it off and hopefully end the Weavers' control," she said. "But getting in there isn't going to be easy."

"I can get in," Opal pointed out.

"But you can't bring the crystal with you through the wall," Charlie said, and Opal deflated. "Listen. You each had an idea, right? Hide, fight, get help. None of them are enough, but we can put them together. Each of you can do something that no one else can, and that means that they won't expect it. Opal, you can hide and walk through walls. That means you can get inside the house without being noticed."

Opal nodded. It was a start.

"Matty, you're fast and fierce. And you're good at making a *whole lot* of chaos," Charlie said. Matty grinned. His eyes were bright amber now. He was going to shift soon, whether he wanted to or not. So they might as well count on it.

"What about me?" Gideon asked.

"I know you don't like to use the psychic part of your powers, but they may be the only shot we've got to contain the people the Weavers have mind-wobbled without hurting them," Charlie said. "You've got to try to mess with the Weavers' control. Keep the mind-wobbled people from doing what they want."

"I don't know. What if I can't?" he asked, fidgeting. "I've never done something like that before."

"You can give it a try, at least—and even if you can't, you'll still be helpful. Just stick with me," Charlie said. "We don't have time to have a complicated, elegant plan. So here's what we're going to do. Opal, sneak inside the house. Unlock the door, and open it for Matty. Matty, get in there and go bananas. Don't get caught, but cause as much destruction as you possibly can to try to draw them out, and *keep running*. Don't attack, okay? Keep them chasing you."

"Fun," Matty said. She could practically see his tail wagging already.

"Then me and Gideon will go in. We go down into the basement. We get Mr. Crispin and the others out, and then I'll use the crystal and blow up whatever weird web thing they've got down there."

"What if they catch us?" Opal asked.

"Then you hide. And Matty fights. And Gideon goes to get help," Charlie said. "Just like you said."

"What about you?" Gideon asked. "You don't have any special powers to protect you."

"Mom says her special power is maturity," Opal said helpfully.

Charlie bit her lip. She thought about what had happened

in the vault with the old woman, and the memory of what had happened with the knife. Maybe they'd been wrong all these years. Maybe there was something special about her, after all. But she couldn't be sure enough to tell them just yet. She took a deep breath. "Listen. I'm your big sister, and I'm supposed to take care of you, and so I'm going to. Powers or no powers."

She tried to sound brave. She thought she even managed it. But inwardly, she was terrified. She was twelve years old, and she was scared out of her mind, but she knew that if she panicked, the others would, too. They had proven themselves. They'd gotten her out of the Malice Vault, all on their own. Now she had to prove herself. She had to keep them safe.

She had to. And so she would.

One way or another.

CHAPTER 19

Baxter was hammering on the door in the basement when they sneaked out the back. Matty had already shifted, but the intelligence behind his eyes was human—for now. His nose twitched rapidly, scenting the air, and he gave a wag of his tail as an all clear as he led them around the side of the house. They crouched next to the hedge in the failing evening light. The street was quiet.

Too quiet.

Charlie pulled binoculars out of the hastily stocked backpack slung over one shoulder. She peered through them at the houses.

Thomas Adebayo was standing in the window of his bedroom. Exactly where he had been the night before when she went to meet Peter. He was wearing the same clothes, too. But now, he wasn't alone. In the downstairs windows, Mr. and Mrs. Adebayo stood, staring outward with the same blank expressions. And down the street, she could see other faces in windows. Some people were standing out on their porches. Many of them had phones in their hands—ready to alert the Weavers, Charlie guessed.

Just as alarming, though, were the people who were missing. She could see Thomas, but Luke was nowhere to be seen. Mr. Crispin wasn't on the front lawn with his wife and daughters, of course. Ms. French was missing, too, three houses down. And the Martins' house was completely dark.

"How are we supposed to get across the street?" Gideon asked after she'd reported what she'd seen.

Charlie bit her lip. Three minutes in and their plan was already in danger. "New plan," she said. She looked at Matty. "We need Freckles."

She explained the new plan quickly. Matty glared at her resentfully the whole time, but didn't object. Not that he really could, since puppies were no better at sign language than spoken English.

At Charlie's signal, Opal flickered out of view and flitted across the street. Charlie could track her movement by the tiny wisps of smoke she shed behind her, but no one else so much as glanced in her direction.

Charlie motioned to Matty. He gave her one last withering look, then tore out from their hiding place. As soon as he reached the street, he started barking and jumping around, biting at imaginary flies before racing a bit farther down the street. There he stopped, wagging his tail and barking, standing right in the middle of the street for all to see. The watchers in the windows turned toward him. He had their attention.

"Okay, Gideon. Remember, they might need a bit of pressure to snap out of it," Charlie said. Gideon nodded. He took a deep breath. He strode out from the side of the house.

"Freckles! Freckles, come here!" he called. He sounded distressed. Maybe it was good acting, but Charlie suspected it was just how he was really feeling. "Freckles!"

Gideon ran toward Matty. Matty bolted away before stopping again, crouched in a play bow, tail wagging furiously. She also suspected that wasn't faked—the sun was setting, and Matty's wolf loved nothing as much as he loved a good game of chase.

More people were watching Gideon and Matty now, but none of them had moved to help. Gideon balled up his fists. The air around him shivered. Charlie heard—no, more like *felt*—a buzzing in her skull.

"I need help right now! My puppy is in the street, and he might get hit by a car! You have to come help me!"

Gideon couldn't make people do things. He wasn't a voice in your mind. It was more like a nudge. A jostle. Enough to make you go, *Wait a minute, what was I doing?*

Or at least it seemed so. Because now people were running toward Matty and Gideon, shouting helpfully to coordinate blocking off "Freckles's" escape routes. Those who weren't moving to help were concentrated on it unfolding.

With everyone's focus on the errant puppy, Charlie strode quickly and confidently across the street. She didn't run. Running would attract too much attention. She walked like she wasn't worried about anything at all.

The whole time, she expected someone to shout or to grab her—but she reached the bottom of the steps. Out of the corner of her eye, she saw Juliana Crispin-Suzuki turn toward her.

Charlie kept her eyes fixed straight ahead. She reached for the door, hoping, hoping—

The door opened before her fingers even brushed the knob, and the smell of thick smoke hit her. Opal, pale and wide-eyed but solid, stood on the other side. Charlie didn't break stride. She walked right through the open door—and through Opal, cold washing over her.

Opal pushed the door shut. Charlie locked it quickly, right as footsteps came up onto the porch. Someone—Juliana, presumably—tried the knob. Charlie fell back from the entrance. Juliana tried the door again, and then the footsteps retreated. Up the street, people were calling out directions to each other, and "Freckles" was still barking and howling happily.

"Well. Here we are," Charlie whispered.

"I found the basement door," Opal whispered back. Charlie flexed her fingers. She'd been clutching the strap of her backpack so tightly her knuckles hurt.

Together, they stole into the kitchen. Charlie checked the time. It had been thirteen minutes since she talked to Pendleton. It seemed impossible that it could have been so quick, but at the same time she felt like she was hurtling along at a million miles an hour with no time to think.

Think things like, *Where the heck are the Weavers? Why aren't they trying to stop us?*

In the dusty kitchen, Opal leaned through a shelf and then back out, nodding. "This is it," she said. Charlie got a grip on the middle shelf and heaved backward. The shelf swung away from the wall easily—there were hidden hinges on the right side. Behind it was a door. She tried the knob. It turned easily. Unlocked.

"That's lucky," Opal said.

Charlie shook her head. "Not lucky. There's no way they would leave something this important unlocked. It's got to be a trap," she said.

"So we don't go down?" Opal asked.

Charlie squared her shoulders. "Trap or not, we have to stop them. And that means we have to go down," she said. She let out a breath. "What are we even *doing*?" she muttered to herself.

"We're being brave," Opal said. And she slipped her hand into Charlie's. It was cool and slight, but it was solid, and Charlie gave Opal a startled look. "Being your sister makes it easier to be real," Opal told her. Charlie's heart cracked open, warmth spilling out. She squeezed Opal's hand, and Opal squeezed back.

Now Charlie felt brave.

Together, they descended into the basement. The stairs were wooden, with peeling gray paint that showed water-damaged wood beneath. With every step, Charlie was sure they were going to splinter and send her plunging through. She envied Opal's weightless descent.

The light from above was barely strong enough to illuminate the dirt floor at the bottom of the steps. Charlie stood there, breathing in damp and dirt smells and waiting for her eyes to adjust.

"There's a light," Opal whispered. She could see better in the dark. She guided Charlie a few steps in. Charlie groped in the air until her fingers caught the chain that connected to a single bare bulb, which flickered on as if annoyed to be asked to work.

The basement wasn't large. A dirt floor, a few posts, cinder block walls. There was an old plastic Christmas tree and some lawn chairs in one corner, but otherwise the room was empty—save for the cocoon of webbing in one corner, like cotton balls mashed together. The small green spiders swarmed on the walls. Near the webbing, they were a single seething mass, but farther away they split into lines, heading off in different directions and vanishing into the seams and cracks in the house.

The sac emanated a strange sound—not really a sound, more of a sensation, like a fingernail scraping against the inside of Charlie's skull. "Do you feel that?" she asked Opal.

Opal nodded, stuttering in and out of visibility. "It makes it hard to stay," she said, clutching at her arms.

"Hold on a little longer," Charlie urged her. There was still no sign of the Weavers. That should be a relief, shouldn't it? So why did she feel so nervous? "I don't see any sign of the people they took, but there's definitely some kind of psychic energy coming from that thing. We can set a small charge, so it just blows up the cocoon. Hopefully that stops the mind-wobbles." Then they could find their missing neighbors and get everyone out.

Charlie swung her backpack around and unzipped it. The alien crystal was inside, along with the control plate. She carefully rotated the small knob on the control plate, setting it so it would blow up the spiders and not the whole house—with Charlie, Opal, and their captured neighbors in it. She stole over as close to the sac as she dared, and stretching out her hands as far as they would go, she settled the crystal into the dirt floor, pressing it down firmly. Then she set the plate against it and ran her fingers along the edge to activate and connect it.

The little display should have lit up with numbers, telling her how long she had to book it before the crystal detonated. Or at least she thought there should be a light or something— but nothing happened. The plate didn't even attach to the crystal. It just fell off. She tried again. It plunked onto the ground.

"What's going on? Did you set it? Do we run?" Opal asked.

"I don't know. Hold on," Charlie said. Frantically, she opened her text messages.

The Operative

8:41 p.m.

How do you make the crystal work??

You found it!

Good job!

Did you like how I hid it?

It's like a present wrapped in a present!

Yes great good but how do you make it work
I have the plate and I'm doing the activation
sequence but nothing's happening

Oh
It's not real

WHY ISN'T IT REAL

I'm not going to give a child a functional
explosive, Charlie
That would be irresponsible
It's just a toy
For playing with
Well the crystal is definitely real
But the control plate isn't

????
HOW IS THAT A TOY

I don't understand the question

I need to blow something up RIGHT NOW what
am I supposed to do

Hmmmm good question
Do you have any other explosives?

IF I DID WOULD I BE USING THE FAKE ONES

Again, the explosive part is very very real

Very very useless

Could use it to prop up a table
Or hold open a door
But yeah not going to explode

THE ONE TIME I NEED YOU TO GIVE ME
SOMETHING ACTUALLY DANGEROUS

"Charlie. Charlie," Opal said, her voice tight with urgency.

"Just a minute, I'm thinking," Charlie snapped.

"Charlie," a voice said, but this time it wasn't Opal. Charlie stiffened. She turned, rising to her feet. Peter was stepping out from the darkness beneath the stairs. There were cobwebs on his shoulders and in his hair.

"Peter. You'd better get back. I'm about to blow this place sky high," Charlie said, trying to sound a lot more confident than she felt.

Peter's head tilted to the side curiously. "No you aren't. You would have done it by now."

In the darkness behind him, something moved. The shape seemed spindly and tall, hunched over in the small space beneath the stairs, but when it emerged from the shadows, it was only Mrs. Weaver, who hardly had to duck. She set a hand on Peter's shoulder, her smile fixed in place and her eyes cold and black. Around her neck, suspended from a chain, was a piece of amber about three inches across, a spider caught inside it. Artifact 818.

"You should have told me your friends were coming, dear," she cooed.

Charlie raised her phone, pulling up the camera. *Click*. The photo flashed on the screen for a moment—Peter, and next to him Mrs. Weaver, eyes blinking along her cheekbones. Then Mrs. Weaver let out a shriek and leaped forward, knocking the phone out of Charlie's hand and wrapping a hand around her throat.

"Rude! Foul little girl," Mrs. Weaver spat at her.

Opal stumbled back, her outline fading as she cried out in terror. Mrs. Weaver's head snapped toward her, the rotation of her neck too smooth to be natural.

"Where do you think you're going?" she asked, and reached out one hand, her thumb and two fingers stretched toward Opal like claws. Abruptly, Opal's fading form popped back into existence, and she staggered, gagging and grabbing at her stomach. Charlie wrenched free of Mrs. Weaver's grasp and lunged toward the stairs. She reached for Opal on instinct, even knowing that she couldn't touch her—but her hand closed around Opal's arm, and they cast each other startled looks.

"Run!" Charlie cried. They didn't have time to figure out what was going on, or what Mrs. Weaver had done to Opal. They dodged around the woman and toward the stairs—just as the light at the top winked out, blocked by a broad-shouldered form. "Agent Baxter," Charlie breathed.

Baxter gave her a stern look. In his arms, held firmly by the scruff of the neck, was Matty, still in wolf form. His lips were peeled back from his teeth, and he was growling, but when he thrashed, Baxter held him firm. "I'm very disappointed in your be-havior, children," Baxter said. He came down the stairs. Charlie fell back against the wall, pulling Opal with her. Holding Opal's arm was odd—it didn't feel like a living girl's, more like the air had gone solid under Charlie's hand. The smoke that had been coiling off her skin since they came down the stairs had disappeared.

Baxter and Matty weren't alone. As soon as Baxter started down the stairs, Mr. Weaver stepped into the doorway, guiding a terrified Gideon in front of him. At the base of the stairs, Matty gave one last great twist of his body, and Baxter released him. Matty hit the ground and scrambled to hide behind Charlie's legs, peering out from behind her with a rumble in his furry chest. Gideon ran past Baxter and wrapped his arms around Charlie's middle. She kept one hand on Opal, the other arm around Gideon, and glared at the adults and Peter.

"Such troublemakers, these two!" Mr. Weaver said with a hearty chuckle, taking his time coming down the stairs.

"I cannot apologize enough for their behavior," Baxter said sorrowfully. Mr. Weaver clapped him on the shoulder.

"Not a problem, neighbor. Not a problem. Why don't you go on upstairs and make sure no one interrupts us?"

"Absolutely," Baxter said. He marched back up the stairs. The door closed behind him, cutting off the shaft of light from the kitchen.

The Weavers smiled. Mr. Weaver's smile was wide and cruel. Mrs. Weaver's smile was fixed and angry. Peter's smile was slight, a smile of habit, trained into him. Charlie glared and tried to feel fierce.

"What are you?" she demanded. "What do you want?"

"We are the web, dear," Mrs. Weaver said. She blinked, and Charlie could *almost* see those other eyes along her cheekbones blink as well.

"As for what we want, why, we don't want anything more than any other good American family," Mr. Weaver said, gesturing expansively. The bare light bulb cast his shadow starkly against the wall. The shadows of his hands seemed stretched out. "To live in a good home. To have friendly neighbors."

"To consume," Mrs. Weaver said, the corners of her mouth sharp as knives. "Like all living things, we must feed. For us, our hunger is not for blood and flesh, root and vine, but for the energy that dwells in the souls of *people*. We can sustain ourselves on the scraps of energy in regular people, but they don't truly satisfy us. They don't nourish us and strengthen us. For that we need special people. People like your mother."

"People like your brothers and sister," Mr. Weaver added. "It's a necessity of our diet, that's all. Otherwise we're very considerate neighbors."

"You eat people. You're monsters. Evil," Charlie said.

"Everything has to eat," Peter said, eyes locked on her. "Your brother turns into a wolf. A carnivore. I'm sure a rabbit would call him a monster, if he hunted it down, but that doesn't make him evil."

"That's not the same thing," Charlie objected.

"Isn't it?" Peter asked. "You're only objecting because this time, you're the rabbit."

"Fine. Then I'm a rabbit," Charlie spat out. "And you? Aren't you a rabbit, too?"

"Maybe," Peter said. "But not forever. My parents take care of me. And when I'm ready, they'll give me gifts like theirs. They'll make me special. Don't you want to be special, too? Like your siblings? Don't you want to matter?"

"I matter," Charlie said, but her voice shook.

"It's nice that they let you think that," Peter said kindly.

"I think that's enough lollygagging," Mr. Weaver said, chipper as ever. He put his hands in his pockets and bounced up on the balls of his feet. "Let's get a move on, kids. Places to go, people to eat, you know how it is!"

Mrs. Weaver beckoned them with a curl of her fingers. "Come this way, children," she said. Opal whimpered. Gideon sucked in a sharp breath. Matty growled.

Charlie stood firm. "We aren't going anywhere with you," she said.

"Come with us, or I will devour your brothers and your sister while you watch," Mrs. Weaver said. Her bright tone never faltered. Gideon flinched against Charlie, and she held him tight. She swallowed. Mr. Weaver was between them and the stairs. And Baxter was up there, anyway. There was nowhere to hide and nowhere to run.

She took Gideon's hand and Opal's. She looked down at Matty. He wouldn't have heard any of the conversation, but one glance at his face told her it didn't matter—the sun must have gone down. He was the wolf, not the boy.

Maybe that was better. Understanding what was happening only made it worse.

She stepped forward, drawing Gideon and Opal with her.

Matty stuck close to them, crouched low against the ground with his ears pinned back against his skull and his tail between his legs. Mrs. Weaver made an approving sound. She and Peter led the way back behind the stairs. At last, Charlie could clearly see the passageway they had used to enter the basement. The edges of it were thick with little spiders. It was round, the floor scooped up at the edges, and it almost looked like it had been *melted* through the ground, rather than dug. At first it was completely dark, and Charlie faltered at the opening, making Mr. Weaver harrumph in annoyance. Then Mrs. Weaver snapped her fingers, and all the spiders on the walls began to glow at once.

The eerie green light washed over them, leaving no shadows. Charlie tried to track how long they had been walking. The corridor was slightly sloped; she was pretty sure they were moving down. It also seemed to curve to the right—like they were slowly working their way down a spiral staircase.

Finally, they reached the end of the long tunnel and stepped out into a cavernous space. The rough stone walls dripped with moisture. Thick webbing was strung across them, and on the webs scuttled spiders—some small like those they'd seen so far, but others much larger. Toward the center of the room, the spiders were as big as Charlie's head. Bigger.

There were cocoons on the walls. Large shapes wrapped entirely in spider silk, like bugs bundled up in a web. The tip of a leather shoe poked out of one. Charlie couldn't tell if the people in the cocoons moving—or breathing—because *everything* seemed to move as the spiders crawled over the webs in an endless seething tide. Intricate lines of webbing connected the cocoons, and all of them seemed to pulse with the same kind of buzzing sound that the smaller cocoon had. As if the smaller one had been like a Wi-Fi router to send out the mind-control signal.

"The parents will be here soon," Mr. Weaver said, entering the room behind them. "Should we devour the children now or save them for later?"

"It would be a shame to spoil our appetites. But on the other hand, an appetizer might be pleasant," Mrs. Weaver mused.

The whole way down the tunnel, Opal's hand had been gradually getting more difficult to hold on to. Now it slipped through Charlie's hand, and the smell of smoke reached her nostrils. She looked down at Opal. Opal looked back, eyes wide.

"Not Charlie, though," Peter was saying. Charlie gave him a sharp look, but he was talking to his parents, not looking her way. "You said that we could take her with us."

Mrs. Weaver's teeth clicked together. "I did say that, didn't I? But that was when you told us that you would keep her out of the way for us."

"You think I would go with you?" Charlie asked, appalled.

As she spoke, she tried to think. The crystal hadn't worked. But it was far from the only destructive force in the Greer household, Charlie thought, an idea forming.

"Opal," Charlie said quietly. The little ghost looked up at her, lip trembling. The air around her was growing hazy. "I know that I should tell you not to be afraid, and not to panic. But I can't. You should be scared. Really, really scared."

Mrs. Weaver chuckled. "A little fear makes a delectable spice."

Opal was staring at Charlie, confusion written in her expression. And then her eyes widened. She nodded once. She fell back a step. Her eyes darted around. She started sucking in quick breaths as she let the fear she'd been fighting wash over her. Charlie grabbed hold of Gideon and Matty's scruff and hauled them back away from Opal as sparks flew in the air around her.

"Oh dear. We can't have that," Mrs. Weaver said. She stretched out her three fingers again—and Matty broke free of Charlie's grip, leaping through the air. His teeth clamped down on Mrs. Weaver's wrist. She screeched and flailed her arm, but Matty hung fast, biting down with all his might. The amber necklace flashed around her neck.

"Gideon, get that necklace!" Charlie shouted.

Gideon stretched out a hand. Charlie's eyes stung, and she coughed as the smoke and sparks eddied around them. Gideon's fingers closed into a fist. The necklace yanked free of Mrs. Weaver's neck, the chain breaking. Peter swiped for it, but it sailed past his fingertips, and Charlie snatched it out of the air.

"It's so loud," Gideon said, his face screwed up in pain. "But I think I can—" He focused furiously. A trickle of blood ran from his nose. Mr. Weaver charged toward Charlie, but in that second the amber shattered.

Charlie whipped her face away as the shards of the amber sprayed in all directions. Mrs. Weaver was screaming; Mr. Weaver was shouting. And Opal let out a high-pitched wail of sheer terror.

They all turned toward the little girl. Her flannel pajamas were gone, replaced by a filmy white nightgown, the hem singed and glowing. Her skin glowed, too, in burning patches that swelled and faded with her breath. Her eyes were like embers, and the storm of sparks around her had turned into an inferno.

She screamed again, a sound that wasn't human at all. Fire rolled across the stone floor around her. It licked the base of the webs on the walls—and they caught, bursting into flame.

Mr. and Mrs. Weaver shrieked, scrambling back away from the flames. Peter stumbled back with them, horror in his eyes.

For the first time, none of the Weavers were smiling.

The fire spread quickly. Charlie looked to the cocoons around the walls. Soon the flames would reach them. She ran to the nearest one, tearing at the sticky silk with her hands. Her fingers plunged into the stuff and touched something hard— an arm, she thought. She grabbed hold and pulled, and Luke Adebayo spilled out into her arms. She put her fingers to his neck, feeling for a pulse.

"He's alive!" she cried. She looked up. Opal was still standing at the edge of the room in the middle of a storm of smoke and flame, her hands in her hair and her mouth stretched in a scream that no longer made any sound at all. Matty was crouched down flat against the floor, a strip of something papery hanging from his teeth. Gideon stood bewildered in the middle of the room, and the Weavers—the Weavers were fleeing. She spotted Peter as he vanished into a tunnel at the far end of the room.

They were going to get away—get away, and get Mom and Dad. Charlie grabbed Gideon's arm. "Gideon! Look at me."

His eyes found hers. He was trembling with fear.

"Gideon, you have to get these people out of here."

"I can't," he said, shaking his head.

"You have to, buddy. You've got this," she said. "Use your powers to carry them out."

"But—"

She pressed a kiss against his forehead. "You can do it. You're a freaking superhero," she told him. She crouched, looking Matty in the eye, and signed deliberately. "Matty. Help Gideon. Get the people out." He looked at her blankly. "Freckles," she tried. She pointed at the cocoon on the wall that had a shoe sticking out of it. "Go get that shoe."

Freckles needed no further instructions. He threw himself at the cocoon, tearing and biting, pulling chunks of silk away. Gideon ran to help, and Charlie turned to Opal. The smoke was thick. She could barely breathe already. Opal flickered in and out of view, jolting a few inches to the right or left each time, her face stretched in mute panic.

"Opal!" Charlie called to her, stretching out her hands. They hit a wall of solid heat, and Charlie recoiled. "Opal, that's enough! You can stop!"

But Opal kept screaming silently, her eyes empty points of light. Charlie gritted her teeth. And she threw herself forward, into the heat. Into the flames. She flung her arms out and wrapped them around where Opal should be, knowing she would pass through her—

But she didn't. Not entirely. For an instant, she felt the slim form of Opal, trembling in her arms. Heard a sharp, startled intake of breath. Heat seared her skin—

And Opal vanished.

This time, the smoke and flame went with her. The webs on the walls were still burning, but the ghost was gone, and with her the source of the fire. Charlie sagged. If she was gone, she was safe. Or so Charlie hoped.

Gideon and Matty had gotten Mr. Crispin out, and Mr. Martin, but there were still three more cocoons. Charlie covered her mouth with her arm, coughing and squinting through the haze of smoke.

"Charlie, go!" Gideon called over his shoulder.

"I can't leave you in here," Charlie choked out, thinking of smoke inhalation and those licking tongues of flame—but then she realized that the air around Gideon was completely clear. The air shimmered with his power, holding the particles of soot and smoke at bay. Charlie felt a flash of pride. Gideon could handle this.

He grinned at her. "We're good. Go save Mom and Dad."

"Get out as soon as you can," she told him. He nodded and turned back to work.

Gideon and Matty didn't need her help. Gideon, against all his instincts, was taking charge. Matty was, if anything, having *fun* tearing open the cocoons.

And Opal—

Opal would be all right. She'd be back, Charlie told herself. The best thing Charlie could do for her was get to Mom and Dad to warn them.

She ran into the tunnel, following the Weavers' path out of the cave.

CHAPTER 20

Charlie ran full tilt. The smoke chased her through the tunnel, but soon enough it faded until the only smoke left was what clung to her skin and scratched at her throat and lungs. The tunnel was dark, but up ahead she could see the faint glow of hundreds—thousands—of fleeing spiders. The tunnel began to slope upward. Then the glow of spiders was replaced by a different light—a streetlight, Charlie realized. She put on a final burst of speed, emerging from a hole in the side of a hill just off the road, near the park.

There was a sign stapled to a wooden stake, driven into the ground just outside the hole. THIS IS NOT A TUNNEL, it read.

Suddenly, a hand closed around her wrist and yanked down—hard. Charlie stifled a yell as she fell backward onto her butt. Peter was crouched down among the bushes, and he pressed his finger to his lips. Charlie started to speak, ready to tell him off—and then she froze. There were clicking sounds coming from around the side of the hill—clicking and rasping, like the not-at-all-human voices she'd heard in the Weavers' house, when she and Peter hid in the closet together what felt like an eternity ago.

"That thing hhhhhurt me. I neeeeeeed to eeeeat something," one horrible, distorted voice said. Mrs. Weaver.

"The meal is closssssse. The bald one issss bringing her," the other voice, which must have belonged to Mr. Weaver, replied. *"We can eeeeat the psychic, and the bald one, and the husss-band. A ttthree-course meal."* He gave a dry chuckle. Charlie crept forward, peering through the bushes. The Weavers—or what she could only assume were the Weavers—were standing a few feet away. They didn't look like people anymore. Mrs. Weaver was much too tall, and eyes blinked and gleamed from not just her cheekbones, but all down her arms. Mr. Weaver's hands were so long they dragged on the ground, and his fingers were like blades. The skin on Mrs. Weaver's forearm hung off her like torn tissue paper. She plucked bits of it off and popped them into her mouth, her jaw moving side to side quickly as she chewed and swallowed. Charlie's stomach roiled with disgust.

"Put yourself back together," Mr. Weaver said. His hands seemed to retract, shrinking down to a normal size. He rolled his neck. Beside Charlie, Peter seemed to relax a fraction.

"I caaaaan't. It huuuuurts and I'm huuunnngry," Mrs. Weaver complained. Mr. Weaver's head turned toward the bush. Toward their hiding place. Peter pressed a hand over his own mouth, as if to hold back any sound.

"You could eat the boy," he said.

Mrs. Weaver made a hissing, growling sound and smacked the back of Mr. Weaver's head. *"No! He'sss my boy. You sssssaid I could have a pet. And he'sssss ussseful."*

"I could get you a new pet. A rat. Or a possum," Mr. Weaver suggested, and chuckled. "Fine, you can keep him. But let's go. We don't want to be late for dinner."

Charlie's heart beat wildly. How could she hope to stop them? She wasn't anything special.

The things in the Malice Vault couldn't even eat her, because there was nothing to eat. She was empty.

It was more than that. She wasn't just an empty cup, where taking a sip would leave you disappointed. She wasn't just *not special*. She was normal. Completely normal.

Extra normal, she thought with a flutter of panicked amusement.

And maybe that was the answer. The old woman in the vault had crumbled to nothing when she tried to feed on Charlie. So maybe that was how she could save her family.

Offer herself up as a snack.

She stood. Peter gasped and grabbed at her, but she stepped free of him. "Stop!" she yelled.

Mr. Weaver wheeled around. His grin was manic. "Oh, look. The little troublemaker has found us." His hand stretched out—and stretched, and stretched, those horribly long fingers reaching impossibly far and closing around Charlie's shoulders. He yanked her forward as she screamed. He held her up, closed in his massive fist.

Charlie wriggled in his grasp. He chuckled again. "I thought I smelled something back there. Peter, come out."

Peter stepped out, shoulders hunched, eyes on the ground.

Mrs. Weaver tilted her hideous face, examining Mr. Weaver's

catch. *"Peter, I told you to leave that thing beeeehind,"* she rasped.

"Please don't eat her," Peter muttered. The Weavers looked at him in apparent surprise. "She could come with us. She could be useful. Like me."

Mr. Weaver seemed to consider. *No!* Charlie thought. She couldn't let them take her with them. She only had one chance to save her parents.

"I won't go with you!" Charlie said, kicking her feet wildly in Mr. Weaver's grasp. "I'll *never* help you. And I won't let you hurt my parents! If you want to get to them, you're going to have to eat me first!"

I really, really hope I'm right about this, she thought, and didn't have to fake the fear on her face.

"Don't listen to her. She'll learn. She'll behave," Peter said, an edge of desperation in his voice. She glanced at him in surprise. He sounded like he truly didn't want her to get hurt. There was an aching look in his face that she knew very well. He hadn't lied when he said he was lonely.

Part of her felt sorry for him. He'd been taken from his family and raised by these monsters.

But now he seemed eager to be a monster himself. She couldn't save him if he didn't want to be saved.

"I will never be your friend. You tried to hurt my family," she told him. "I hate you. I will always hate you. You're a monster."

His jaw tensed. "Fine," he said. "I tried to help you. This is your fault." He looked over at Mr. Weaver. "You can eat her."

Mr. Weaver smiled widely. "Appetizer it is." His mouth

stretched open. He leaned toward her, his eyes lighting with the same greenish glow as the spiders, and Charlie felt something cold and prickly against her skin, and then a sharp pain. It was like the pain of a needle sliding in, but not in any particular spot—more like a needle going into her *soul*.

Mr. Weaver's eyes widened, but it was too late. She could feel the *tug* inside her, and then a faint pop and a rushing cold as the greasy, sticky extranormal energy inside Mr. Weaver rushed into the void of Charlie's absolutely ordinary self and instantly evaporated.

He let out a gasp. His hand went slack. Charlie fell to the ground in a crouch. Mrs. Weaver screeched in horror as his limbs began to wither, his flesh pulling tight against his bones like a mummy, like the woman on the wardrobe. His limbs pinched up next to his body, and a puff of dust flew from his mouth in one last cough before he toppled over, hitting the ground with a clatter.

Charlie stared at the withered husk of the thing that had been Mr. Weaver as bits of ash flaked off and flurried away in the breeze. Mrs. Weaver stared. Peter stared. The body began to crumble, turning to fine dust, until all that was left was a scattering of fluffy gray powder.

Charlie raised her eyes to Mrs. Weaver.

"*Whhhhaaaat aaaaare youuuuu?*" Mrs. Weaver demanded, recoiling.

Charlie smiled. "I'm just a nice, normal girl, Mrs. Weaver," she said. She advanced a pace. Mrs. Weaver fell back.

"*Donnn't touch me*," she said. She retreated again, horror on her face. Charlie flexed her fingers. The woman on the wardrobe, Mr. Weaver—they'd done that to themselves by trying to feed on her. But maybe she could do it on purpose. She was pretty excited to find out.

"Get out of here. Get out and never come near my family again, or I'll do even worse to you!" Charlie warned.

"*Peterrrr! Rrrrrun*," Mrs. Weaver screeched, scrambling back.

Peter started after her. At the last second, Charlie reached out, caught his sleeve. "Don't go with her!" she cried. "Peter. You don't have to be like them." But Peter shoved her, tearing free, and sprinted after the creature he called his mother.

Charlie sank down to her knees, watching as the two figures disappeared into the distance—running away from the neighborhood. Away from her family.

She should get to her feet. She should go make sure Gideon and Matty had gotten everyone out, find her parents, find *Opal*—

But she was too tired. All she could do was stare off into the dark as the dusty remains of Mr. Weaver scattered in the wind.

CHAPTER 21

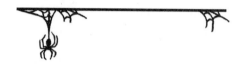

Nearby, sirens wailed. The smell of smoke wafted toward her on the breeze.

"Charlie!" a voice called.

Charlie stiffened. That was her father's voice.

"Charlie, where are you?" her mother called.

She struggled to her feet. They couldn't be here. What if Mrs. Weaver came back? She staggered toward the street. In the distance, the Weavers' house was on fire, flames leaping from the windows as firefighters sprayed them. The whole neighborhood seemed to have gathered outside to watch, some of them wandering around in bewildered confusion.

Charlie's parents were standing in the street. Charlie walked toward them. She tried to call out, but her exhaustion and the lingering smoke made her cough instead.

Her mother saw her first. She grabbed her husband's arm to get his attention, then sprinted down the road toward Charlie. They reached her in the same moment.

"Charlie! Are you okay? Look at me, sweetheart," her mother said, hands cupping her face.

"You can't . . . it's not safe," Charlie said weakly.

"It's okay. We know what's going on," her dad said.

"Gideon. And Matty. They were in the house," Charlie said frantically, starting toward the burning building as she remembered, but her dad caught her.

"They're fine. They got everybody out. They're with Baxter at the house," he said.

"But Baxter is—"

"Extremely embarrassed," her dad said. "But not mind controlled anymore. Everybody's snapped out of it."

"And Opal—"

"We found her in her room. She went back to where she felt safe," Mom said, and at the words, a sob escaped Charlie's lips.

Dad put both his hands on her shoulders, looking her in the eye. "You did it. Really. It's over, Charlie."

She looked between them. "It's over?"

"No more bad guys," her mom promised her, and pulled her in for the biggest, warmest Leigh Greer hug that Charlie had ever felt. Charlie sank into her, letting the calm of the Soothe wash over her, chasing away the fear and the anger and the hurt.

When her tears stopped and she had caught her breath, Charlie straightened up. She peered past her mother. There were a number of men and women in black suits with extremely serious expressions who were walking around and collecting up the neighbors one by one, escorting them back to their houses.

"Are those . . . ?" Charlie started.

"A.D.E.P.T. showed up to lend a hand," Dad said.

"How did they know something was wrong?" Charlie asked.

"They monitor the Operative's texts," Dad said. "Apparently you were asking some alarming questions." He arched an eyebrow at her.

"Oh. Right," Charlie said, cheeks flushing.

"I knew I should have checked that doll," Dad muttered. He put his hands on his hips, surveying the chaotic scene. "Charlie, this—this is incredible. You figured all of this out on your own?"

"Gideon and Matty and Opal helped," Charlie said, wiping at her cheeks with the back of her hand. "Opal helped me sneak into the house, and Matty and Gideon got me out of the Malice Vault, and Assistant Director Dixon told me about the Portland case, and—"

"We've been after these things for years, and you solved it before the end of the weekend," her dad said, looking impressed. Then his face grew serious. "Not that you should have."

Charlie's mom tucked her hair back behind her ear. "Sweetheart, what were you thinking? You should have called us right away."

"I know," Charlie said, voice wobbling. "But you needed the break. I know you did. I heard you say you couldn't keep doing this, and you didn't know how you could keep going, and I don't want you to be sad all the time, and it's my job to take care of things—I know I'm not special, but I can protect the family, I can, even without powers, like you said, Dad . . ." She was babbling, and tears welled up in her eyes. She scrubbed them away furiously.

Her parents exchanged a long, strained look. "Charlie, I didn't mean you had to carry the weight of the whole world on your shoulders," her dad said. "You don't need powers. And you don't need to protect your family all by yourself. You're a kid. I never meant . . ." He ran a hand through his hair and looked helplessly at Mom.

"We're grown-ups, Charlie. We get stressed. And it's our job to deal with that, not yours," her mom said. "Good lord. And I thought we were getting pretty good at this parenting thing."

"You're really good parents," Charlie said quickly, grabbing her mom's hand.

"Who apparently have been putting way too much pressure on you," she replied, and kissed Charlie's hair. "Oh, my love. My incredible, amazing, brilliant girl. You are really something special. I hope you know that."

"Sometimes it's hard to believe," Charlie admitted, and her voice broke. Her dad dropped down to one knee and pulled her and her mom in close. She shut her eyes, burrowing against him.

There was a shout from up the street, and Charlie looked up to see Gideon hurtling toward them, Matty loping at his heels. She grinned and opened one arm as Gideon joined the hug, followed quickly by a furiously wiggling wolf pup who squirmed into the middle of the pile.

A wisp of smoke danced around them, then twisted down toward the ground. Opal appeared, pearlescent and shimmering. Charlie stretched out one hand. Opal reached out, palm to palm, and a little line formed between her brows. Charlie felt the cool skin of Opal's palm, and they twined their fingers together.

They were together. And that meant that whatever happened, everything was going to be okay.

They stayed like that for a long moment. And then a voice spoke.

"Excuse me. The director would like a word." A towering man in a black suit had approached them, standing at a distance with his hands folded loosely in front of him.

Mom straightened up. Dad broke away from the hug. "Right, of course," Dad said, but the man shook his head.

"She'd like to speak to your daughter," he said, nodding to Charlie. Behind him, a sleek black limo pulled up beside the curb. The back door opened. Charlie gulped.

"Better go see what she wants," Dad said, tipping his head toward the car and looking resigned.

"We'll be right here," Mom said with a reassuring smile.

The man in the black suit beckoned. Charlie marched forward, feeling like she was going to her own funeral. She clambered inside the limo, finding herself sitting opposite a woman in a steel-gray pantsuit, her red-blond hair pulled back in a severe bun. She was a woman who radiated all the warmth of an icicle, and her gaze was similarly likely to put out an eye.

"Charlotte Greer," Director Winter said, her hands folded on one leg, her gaze stern. "I trust that you have an explanation for all of this."

"All of what, exactly?" Charlie asked, knowing from long experience that it's best not to admit to anything until you're sure the other person already knows.

Director Winter fixed her with a flat look. "Let me see if I have this right. New neighbors moved in. Upon realizing that they were suspicious, rather than alerting any sort of authority or adult, you took it upon yourself to work out what they were. Then, upon having identified them as people-eating monsters who have successfully evaded all attempts to stop or apprehend them for decades, you decided to take them on by yourself."

"Not by myself. Matty and Opal and Gideon helped," Charlie objected.

"Yes. A six-year-old ghost, a telekinetic with allergies, and a half-grown werewolf. Not exactly professionals," Director Winter said.

"Hey, we did a great job," Charlie said defensively.

Director Winter raised an eyebrow. "You are very lucky, Charlie, that my agents are here to clean up the mess you left behind. Those neighbors who were victims of the Weavers are being transported to the hospital for treatment, and A.D.E.P.T. is hard at work doing our usual job of making sure that no one has any notion of what's happened here the last few days."

"What are you going to tell people happened?" Charlie asked.

Director Winter waved a hand. "Gas leak, probably. Dull, perhaps, but it's a classic for a reason. And it explains the raging inferno quite handily. Opal's work, I hear."

"I hope she's okay," Charlie said. "She was so scared."

Director Winter's expression softened. "Opal will be fine, Charlie. She was scared, but she was also quite brave. And she knew that she had a safe home to return to. She has come a long way. I don't think that we need to worry about losing her anymore."

Charlie wiped away a tear at the corner of her eye, trying to hide her sniffles. Director Winter leaned forward, holding out a handkerchief, and Charlie accepted it wordlessly.

"Now, I think that I am aware of most of what happened here. Except for the very end. What happened after you chased the Weavers into the tunnel?" Director Winter said.

Charlie bit her lip. "I'm not sure," she admitted. "I caught up to the Weavers. Mr. Weaver wanted to eat me, but when he tried, he sort of . . . dried up and turned to dust?"

Director Winter made a soft, satisfied sound. "I thought as much," she said. "Charlie, you aren't just *not* supernatural. You are completely normal. Aggressively so. So much so that your absolute lack of anything even a little bit supernatural can actually destroy extranormal energy."

Charlie looked at her in alarm. "I destroyed Mr. Weaver. What if I did that to Matty or Gideon or Opal? What if—"

Director Winter held up a hand. "The only reason Mr. Weaver was destroyed was that he tried to feed on you. I promise you won't accidentally turn your siblings into tidy piles of dust, however tempted you might be at times. This isn't a weapon you can wield or an ability you can train. It's just what you are."

"It happened in the Malice Vault, too. Today, but also years ago. Right?" Charlie asked.

"The knife," Director Winter said, sounding satisfied. "We'd tried for many years to find a way to destroy it, and all it took was one night in a room with a terrified six-year-old to turn it into so much dust. I wasn't completely sure how it had happened until now, but I've suspected for a long time."

Charlie gave her an accusatory look. "You knew and you didn't tell me?"

"I keep secrets professionally," Director Winter reminded her. "There was no strategic advantage in telling you. So I didn't."

"Great. Thanks," Charlie grumped, but Director Winter only looked amused.

"Charlie, I understand wanting to take care of your family," she said. "But part of keeping your family safe is knowing when to ask for help. You should have contacted me."

"You deleted your contact from my phone," Charlie said.

"As if that would stop you if you really wanted to get a hold of me," Director Winter said, a gleam of challenge in her eyes.

"Maybe I didn't want to bother you," Charlie said.

"I'm your godmother. It's all right to bother me in case of mortal peril," Director Winter said. She shook her head. "You are so much like Leigh sometimes. Leaping off into danger without a second thought. Taking on all the troubles of the universe as if it's your job to handle everything by yourself."

Charlie hid a smile. "You know, everyone always says I take after my dad. They never compare me to Mom."

"That's because most people are fools who can't see past their own noses. They think because you aren't extranormal, you must be more like your father. I'm afraid you've inherited his stubbornness and Leigh's total lack of self-preservation." The tiniest hint of a smile curled the corner of her mouth.

Someone rapped on the window. Director Winter leaned over and rolled it down, revealing Leigh Greer, bent over and waving. "Hi. Hello there. Agatha. Do you think I could have my daughter back, or are you going to whisk her away to some secret facility in Antarctica?"

"Don't be ridiculous. The Antarctic facility is hardly a secret," Director Winter said, and winked at Charlie. "You can have your daughter back. But Leigh?"

"Yes, Aggie?" Mom asked sweetly.

"There are very few things in this world I allow myself to truly care about. You and your family are on a very short list. Which is why I must say, with love, that you are unbearably overworked and you, your marriage, and your children are suffering for it. A.D.E.P.T. will be in touch regarding a proposal to lighten the Division's workload. I suggest you give it serious consideration."

Mom sighed. "I will," she promised. She opened the door; Charlie stepped out. The limo pulled away as soon as the door closed. Charlie's dad approached. They watched the flames leap from the Weavers' roof. Mom put an arm around Charlie's shoulders. Dad stuck his thumbs through his belt loops. Gideon took Charlie's hand. Opal stood next to Gideon. Matty pressed himself against Charlie's shins.

"Everybody's home," Opal said, sounding satisfied.

"Everybody's home," Charlie agreed. "And everything's going to be okay."

They were together.

They were the Greers.

And they would figure it out.

ACKNOWLEDGMENTS

Every book brings its own delights and struggles, but *Extra Normal* has proved to be the rare book that was nearly all delight from start to finish. Charlie, Matty, Opal, Gideon, the Greer parents, Agents Pendleton and Baxter, and the incorrigible Miss Sinister were a bright spot in one of the most difficult years of my life. It is a true joy to see them alive on the page at last. Many people helped me to bring their story to readers. In no particular order, a huge thanks to everyone who had a hand: Mike Marshall, Shanna Germain, Erin M. Evans, Susan Morris, Rhiannon Held, Corry L. Lee, and Rashida Smith; my agent, Lauren Spieller; illustrator Matt Rockefeller; and the team at Viking and Penguin Young Readers, Maggie Rosenthal, Maria Fazio, Kaitlin Kneafsey, Anabeth Bostrup, Marinda Valenti, Krista Ahlberg, Alicia Lea, and Camilla Kaplan.

Special thanks as well to Boomer, who was not an evil cat, just a bad one.